PRAISE FOR R.J. JOSEPH

"RJ writes with a style that is both literary and accessible, emotive yet direct."

BEN YOUNG

"Left Hand Torment was absolutely mind-shattering for me. That's the only one that honestly, gave me nightmares; it was so terrifying, hauntingly vivid, and brutal. I thoroughly enjoyed it…raw, more than viscerally violent content. It is definitely hardcore horror; these are the kinds of [stories] women in horror are sometimes accused of being too dainty in our sensibilities and sensitive to write."

SUMIKO SAULSON, EDITOR OF BLACK MAGIC
WOMEN

"[*The Collector* is] one of the darkest stories I've ever read. Still a bit shook."

THOMAS GLOOM

My Monsters Ain't Like Yours

A COLLECTION OF SHORT STORIES

R.J. JOSEPH

MY MONSTERS AIN'T LIKE YOURS

A COLLECTION OF SHORT STORIES

R.J. JOSEPH

My Monsters Ain't Like Yours
written by R.J. Joseph
published by Quill & Crow Publishing House

Edited by Mathew Reyes, Cassandra Thompson

Printed in the Unites States of America.

ISBN: 978-1-967911-18-9

ISBN: 978-1-967911-17-2 (ebook)

quillandcrowpublishinghouse.com

Dedicated to the bright lights that destroy my personal monsters: Josè and our beautiful babies. Shine on, my radiant beloveds.

PUBLISHER'S NOTE

Please be advised that this book includes themes that may prove triggering for some, including sexual assault, child abuse, and historical accounts of slavery and racism. For a full list, please refer to the Trigger Index in the back of the book.

ONE
THE CRAZY WITH DAISY

I love my best friend in the Universe, but she always drove me nuts, like, beyond anything I'd ever experienced in my whole life.

My crazy Daisy wanted me to be crazy with her, even when she knew what she was doing was dangerous—and I obliged more often than I declined. I couldn't refuse her anything. Like the time she grabbed my hand and we ran away from a taxi driver without paying because she said the woman had insulted us. She had, and was pretty ugly about it, too—but we also had ridden in her cab with the agreement that we pay for her service. I was just glad Daisy hadn't also hauled off and punched the woman, as she sometimes did to folks who crossed us.

Then there was the time she bought us those edibles from some chick she knew and we stayed high as shit for two days straight because there was no content label on the brownies and she didn't ask. We had fucked up a dude who grabbed Daisy's ass in an alley when we went on our fourth munchies run, and I'd never loved her more than in those moments when she dragged my blade swiftly across his bare stomach as I held his ass down and punched him in the head. He'd forever wear that D+J she'd engraved in him.

But she may have topped her list of crazy on our walk through the cemetery that one day.

Really, what happened was partially my fault because I made the mistake of saying my thoughts out loud where she could really hear them. We were super close and all, and she could sometimes read my mind. She probably wouldn't have picked up on my curiosity from that day without me verbalizing it.

We walked through the old Lafayette Cemetery No. 1 every other Sunday afternoon when we made the drive from Houston to visit my granny for the weekend. Always in the daylight hours, because Granny insisted it was the only almost safe time to do it, if we just had to. And we just had to.

"Ain't no good coming outta that place," she'd admonish, every single time we left. "Not too much good going in, either." She usually spat a thick, brown stream of snuff-tinged spittle into her spit cup at this point, to punctuate just how she felt about the graveyard being the final resting place of the family who had owned ours as slaves. She'd spit again, the ongoing memory as foul as the tobacco product she'd dipped her whole life.

"They robbed our lives then, and there's devils and stuff waiting to rob you now. If y'all gotta go, go and come back real quick, while the sun's still up."

We'd kiss her and agree to be back before dark. As peaceful as the cemetery always was, I wasn't trying to see what these devils she religiously mentioned were all about. She never offered any more explanation, and we never asked.

Besides, I was carrying my own beloved devil, Daisy, right along with me. She never hesitated to raise some kind of hell.

The innocently spoken thought that unleashed the devilment that day was, "I wonder what those mausoleums look like on the inside."

I had seen a large crack in one of the ornate little death houses, and it triggered my insatiable curiosity. It looked old, and it sat right in the middle of hurricane central, so a crack was no huge deal. But I'd never seen the inside of one in real life.

Daisy squeezed my hand and wrinkled her nose. She was cute. And she loved me. I loved her, too, but I didn't want to take our perfect friendship to the next level. We had fifteen years of history and were still inseparable. I felt like adding a sexual aspect would likely ruin that. Neither of us could keep a lover, and although we still had all the intimacies as any other couple, I was willing to ride along like that just to keep her close—even if she and Granny insisted we were soulmates and should just get on with the loving already.

"Hmmmm. I don't know," she answered. "Why would you want to go inside, with all this dead smell around us?"

"Yeah, just about everything here is dead. That's what this place is for, right?"

She suddenly dropped my hand. I thought she was testy at me teasing her. She got a little bristly sometimes, and I really dug it. That didn't mean I tried to evoke that kind of response from her on purpose. Well, not often. Certainly not right there, right then.

Suddenly, she was gone. I spun around to find her with her head stuck halfway down inside an even larger crack some ways away, that I hadn't seen.

"Dammit, Daisy! You're being peak white girl right now with this crazy shit! Get from outta there before something drags your skinny ass through that hole!" I stalked toward where she stood on one tiptoe, going further down the hole. "You know what Granny said! Get your tail down from there! I ain't taking my Black ass down there to get you, either, when you fall."

Then she was gone, gone. Like, all the way down the hole, leaving one sandal propped against the bottom of the mausoleum after it dropped from her foot.

I stuck my face to the hole, trying in vain to get my shorter, rounder body up closer and higher. "Daisy!'

I could hear her screaming on her way down...to where? How far?

"Fuck, fuck, fuck! I'm coming, girl!" I didn't know how I was going to get down there, but I was determined, regardless of all the shit I had talked about not going to save her. I couldn't live without her.

I ran along the sidewalk on the row of crypts, where I could still hear her muffled sobs and screams. I followed them to some bushes behind one of the older units. There, in the brambles, was a hole in the ground, much larger than the crack Daisy had fallen...been pulled?...through. Large enough to accommodate my hips and thighs.

"Daisy!" I clambered down through the hole, trying to keep the thorns on the bushes from scratching my face while I held tightly to my cell phone. The deeper I went, the more quickly the signal went out. I probably should have called 911 before I headed down, but I hadn't had that presence of mind. What the hell kind of place was I headed to that cut out cell phone signals?

I landed at the bottom of the hole after several moments of sliding down the slick dirt. The path was well worn, although it was also well hidden. I took some time to try to let my eyes adjust and listened for Daisy again. All I had to go on was whimpers that stabbed at my heart. She was full of spit and vinegar, my Daisy. If she was whimpering, she was really scared.

And that pissed me off.

I turned my flashlight app on, and the rays landed on slimy walls with just enough space between me and them for me to turn around. It looked just like any other nightmarish set of tunnels I'd ever seen on television, but slimier. And stinkier. The smell wasn't quite like death, but more like the lingering of decay you might get from something rotting slowly but surely.

When I heard the muffled sounds of struggle coming from a tunnel on my right, I headed that way. "Daisy!" I lowered my usually loud voice to a stage whisper, pretty sure whatever had her could hear me, too, but still wanting her to know I hadn't abandoned her.

I made my way toward the noise as quickly as I dared go with the slick ground beneath me and the jagged edges of tree roots and random pieces of bone and wood jutting out from the walls around me. I grabbed a funky, patterned piece of fabric off one of the bones, and fear gripped my bowels.

The patch was from the pants Daisy was wearing, which matched my blouse. Granny was always giving "her girls," as she affectionately called us, items from her wardrobe that she decided she was too seasoned a woman to wear anymore. That particular set was one of her favorites. Daisy had the height to pull off Granny's pants, where I had the breasts to fill out her blouses. Granny was especially tickled when we left that day in our matching, gifted set.

"I love to see a couple all dressed alike!" Her guffaws followed us through the cluttered front foyer of her little cottage.

"Granny, we ain't a couple. We're just homegirls," I reminded her.

At the same time, Daisy contradicted me. "Granny, she can't fight us forever when we look this good together in our 'fits!"

They both had laughed, a sound that always filled me with happiness when coming from the two people I loved most in the world. I had to find Daisy, and we both had to get out of that place okay. What would happen to Granny if I died or became injured?

What would happen to me and Granny if Daisy did?

That thought spurred me on a little faster until I almost tripped. I heard the harsh breathing down below, where I originally had the flashlight turned upward. I trained the beam of light at my feet and couldn't quite comprehend what I saw until I saw Daisy, hands outstretched towards me, silent, face soaked in tears.

"Are you okay? We gotta get outta here." I reached down to help her up, and she grasped at my hands with one of hers but pointed with the other. I didn't immediately look where she pointed. Instead, my brain registered that I must have stumbled over something other than Daisy. I looked down, and at my feet lay a small figure.

I thought it might be a dog or something, but it was covered in blood and had really short hair covering its body, the kind you saw on super hairy people who weren't supposed to have that much hair but did. It was also humanoid. I could then make out a head, or something mangled where the head would have been, a torso, and three appendages, much like ours. It wasn't quite child-sized. Maybe toddler-sized?

It wasn't no human toddler. Not human at all.

The things Daisy pointed towards weren't, either.

A group of the creatures huddled away from the rays of the flashlight. They varied in size, mostly comparable to the one Daisy obviously had killed with her 70s goth disco boots. I always knew her fashion sense would help us out in big ways one day, other than getting us into the good clubs.

Some were a bit larger than those—very few were smaller. All had some variation of the short hair covering their otherwise naked bodies. Wide set, slitted eyes sat on either side of their faces, shut against the bright light I shone at them. It started to register that some of them had ears and others didn't. Some had various body parts either missing or misshaped. Further investigation revealed that wasn't the worst thing about them.

Two stepped forward from the crowd, and the human hand on the largest one was noticeable at first glance. The desiccated fingers moved slowly, the creak from the dried joints almost audible. The other apparent leader dragged a human foot behind it, toes wiggling slowly as it helped paddle the body forward.

"What the actual fuck?" My mouth fell open, and I dragged Daisy up toward me. It was really time to go when I saw the human breasts jaggedly sewn onto the front of another one of the creatures, with a smaller one nuzzling and suckling one of them.

"Turn off the light. It hurts us." The voice came the short way across the cavern, gritty and guttural, but clear.

"Bullshit. I'm keeping the light, and you gonna let us go." I released Daisy's hand just long enough to grab my switch blade from where I kept it tucked in my bra. "Fight us, and we gonna be rocking and rolling in this bitch. Move!"

Daisy regained her bravado and soon brandished both her boots, heels out, pointed towards our blockade.

Another spoke. "We need more parts to make us whole. We need your parts."

The longer I looked at them, the more evidence of their plastic surgery I saw, whether I wanted to or not.

"Why would we just let you kill us and take our parts? You got us fucked up."

"We are almost extinct. Disease and rot have taken more of us than we can afford to lose. Some of us can no longer bear and feed our young. We will not perish."

"We ain't perishing, either." Daisy issued her warning down low from her throat.

"There are no longer any new bodies being buried here, so we have to catch humans when we can. We caught you. You will not escape."

"Good luck with that." I swung the blade around wildly, flashing the light as widely as I could.

"There are more of us behind you and surrounding you on all sides."

The musty smell in the space had increased, so I knew it spoke truth. Still, Daisy and me were gonna go down fighting. We were ride or die, and that didn't change when we just might really die after riding.

Something charged me from my right side, banging hard into my thigh as I barely caught sight of a fuzzy head covered with a human skull forehead ramming me. I slashed my blade across the human ear it wore, and it howled in pain and fell back. Daisy was busy on my other side, swinging her boots and connecting with wet thuds into solid bodies.

We fought them off as best we could before we both realized there were more of them than us. We were doing some damage, but it wouldn't be enough. They had too many reinforcements. We huddled together, back-to-back, and Daisy whispered over her shoulder.

"We gotta do something different."

I had no other ideas. Then I heard her speak, and in that moment, I wasn't sure I wanted her to because I had no idea what she would say.

"Wait!" she yelled. She repeated her command, and the movement in the hole paused. One of the leaders held up their hand, and the others stopped their attacks.

"We can help you get parts."

I swiveled my head around to stare at her. "Girl…"

"No, really. You say the light hurts you, so you obviously can't go hunting in the daytime. We can. And we can bring you people so you don't have to endanger yourselves doing it. In return, you let us go, and you never hurt us."

"How many people?"

I couldn't believe they were entertaining this bargain. But if the crazy shit got us out of there, I had to entertain it, too.

"We can't just go around snatching everybody who comes in here. If we're discovered, it's the end for us and you."

"Can we get one every time you visit here? We have been watching you. We know you come every fourteen days of sun."

That tightness in my gut came back, replacing the fight or flight in me. *They had been watching us? For how long?*

"Deal. But you can never hurt us again. Ever. Or else, we reveal where you are and send somebody to really exterminate you."

"You had better keep your end of our bargain, as well. You can never hide from us." It looked directly at me. "We also keep watch on your beloved Granny. If you fail us, her parts will be distributed among us first of all. After her, we will find you."

Granny would never leave her New Orleans to get out of their grasp. They were already watching. Granny apparently knew more about these things than she had told us. We had to keep her safe.

Daisy looked at me, and we locked eyes. I nodded.

"Okay. Now let us out of this stinkhole."

"One more thing. We will need a replacement for you, for today. You must bring us the first before you leave."

I became frantic. "How do you expect us to just do that on the fly like that? With no prior preparation?"

"You had better figure it out, or we will take you both back before you can leave here. We are legion."

Daisy took my hand that time. "Fine. Whatever. Let us go so we have time to figure this out."

The crowd parted, and we could see a ray of light coming from up above the tunnel behind them. I continued to flash my cell phone in their direction, blade still in hand, as Daisy took the lead and ran towards our escape.

I expected the creatures to rush us from behind. But they didn't. We emerged on a different side of the cemetery just as the sun was setting.

The first thing I did after we ran far away from the hole was grab Daisy and press her against the nearest crypt. She didn't fight my embrace or the fevered kiss I pressed to her mouth. She returned my passion, and soon, our breath was coming in jagged rushes.

"I love you, you crazy ass girl."

"Well, shit. All it took was for us to be attacked by monsters and to make a murderous pact with them to make you decide to commit?" She looked into my eyes. "This is finally a commitment, right?"

"It sure is. I think it's a requirement to commit to somebody when you make a pact to murder with them." I'd tell her later how sexy her whole proposal had been. Even when I had thought we might not make it out of that hole alive, I had been massively turned on hearing her suggest we go on a long-term killing spree together. I didn't hate the idea.

If that didn't show we were twin flames, nothing would.

We could hear the vestiges of a heated conversation coming our way from between the crypts.

"Stop it! I wanna leave. I don't like it here. Let me go!" The voice was pleading with someone who, apparently, wasn't listening. Daisy and I moved quietly to where the couple stood behind a row of the small stone buildings, the speaker down on the ground underneath the assailant.

"You know you want this. Just shut up."

I looked at Daisy, and she held her hand out toward the couple, inviting me to move in first.

"Hey." I met the gaze of the person on the ground. "Everything okay?" Terrified eyes met mine, and they shook their head in fright.

"Why don't you mind your own business." The attacker turned his head toward us and then smiled. "Oh, maybe not. Why don't you join us? I can do all of you bitches real quick."

'Why don't you let them go and come play with us, instead?" Daisy turned her signature head tilt on him, and he was a goner. To be fair, the head tilt always worked on me, too. It was delicious.

Dude was like that little dog with the bone who was willing to let his trapped prey go at the promise of a bigger prize in Daisy and me. He got up off the victim he held down, and they scrambled up and ran out of the cemetery, without looking back.

I was glad there was no witness. Our new partners hadn't specified whether they wanted the victims dead or alive, so we opted to slice his tongue out and cut his hamstrings before shoving him down the hole. That way, we could get a little blood and still leave him alive for whatever they wanted to do with him. And he couldn't scream or run. I really liked that part.

After we were done with our first job, my blood swirled around inside my body until I thought I'd bust. The sun was well on its way down, but we no longer feared the place after dark. We now knew what devils lurked there, and we had some modicum of protection.

But as we walked toward home, I told Daisy, "Granny got some explaining to do."

She giggled and pulled my hand into her shirt and onto her breast. "So do you, my darling Janay. So do you."

TWO
WHERE THE HORIZON KISSES
THE SKY

The normally sure-footed and nimble, voted "Most Likely to Join a Professional Track Team" in high school Naomi face-planted over the tree roots she didn't see on her regular morning run.

She stood up and dusted off her hands, glad she didn't feel any injuries. "Where did those come from?"

The roots hadn't been there the previous day. Naomi had run or walked that isolated route in the East Texan piney woods at the outskirts of town pretty much every day since high school thirty years prior. She knew the paths the same way she knew the wrinkles that appeared weekly in her face. Every time there was a change in her forest, however gradual, she noticed it.

This change hadn't been gradual.

She poked at the huge roots with her sneakered foot, gently brushing the freakishly long grass that had already grown up around them. *What was that?* Naomi brought her gaze up along the trunk attached to the weird roots and gasped. The trunks were covered in scales, unlike the patches of bark that covered the other evergreens. A hint of yellow beneath the gray made the large stems look almost like chicken legs. Naomi looked up, puzzled, directly into the eyes of an older woman standing in a doorway at the top of the legs.

"Well, stop being rude and get on up here, gal. May as well get all in my business up inside my house since you investigating all outside."

Mortified to have been caught staring, Naomi took one step back —right into a wooden lift made of intertwined tree branches that closed as soon as she was inside. The lift flew upward and deposited Naomi inside what was supposed to be the belly of the chicken, but was instead an almost regular-looking cabin. *Almost.*

Despite herself and forgoing all her impeccable Southern manners, Naomi gawked at the abode. The cabin was made of windows all around, visible from the outside and below as three solid walls. She shivered as she gazed out the side that featured a frozen wasteland, wind whipping everywhere, blowing snow and ice throughout. She tried to focus on the small structure in the far distance, but was distracted by the rays of heat coming through the second wall of glass.

Naomi walked over to the display and pressed her hand to glass that was extremely warm to the touch. Beyond were expanses of sand, a molten desert with ripples where the wind took pity and blew for a long, slow moment as she watched. Again, she squinted and looked toward a tiny speck in the midst of the grains, unable to quite make out what it was that called to her through that window, just at the edge of the scene, where the horizon kissed the sky.

"You done? Wanna tell me about this man of yours you pining over so you're tripping over your own feet?"

Naomi turned around, grasping for pearls she wasn't wearing. "Wh-what do you mean?"

How did the woman know her thoughts?

"Oh, I know a lot. About a whole lot. Ain't no secrets from me around here. No, siree." The woman was older than Naomi had first thought. She couldn't place her exact age, though. Surely, she was too wizened to stretch her arms as far as she did across the cabin— several feet—to grab a chair and pull it close to where Naomi stood. *Surely.*

"Sit. Can't help you if you don't tell me what you want. You gotta say it."

Naomi supposed she should be frightened by the strange woman and her stranger ways. She would've thought she was drunk, but she didn't drink. And, though she might need reading glasses soon, her eyesight wasn't afflicted, either. She was seeing the woman, clear as day. She saw the woman's every move just as clearly.

And something made her sit in that strangely offered chair. She wasn't drawn to it in the same way she was drawn to the scenes outside the woman's windows, but drawn to sit, nonetheless.

"I…I'm not sure what you want me to say." Honesty seemed the best way to go. Things definitely couldn't get any more weird—or so she thought.

The elder woman cackled, and even though Naomi heard her raspy delight in her ears and all around her, the woman's neck stretched to the far corner of the room, now twice as large as it had been when Naomi first arrived. The gnarled hand that had moved the chair Naomi sat in crossed the slender, berobed torso, and picking up a mortar and pestle, she began to work with the single appendage.

"You gotta say it," she repeated.

Naomi felt tears sting behind her eyes. She twisted her hands in her lap, intertwining her fingers in a mimicry of the way the other woman twisted the fingers of her other hand—*her third hand?*— around various ingredients she added to her concoction.

"I don't think my husband loves me anymore, and I don't know what to do about that. I keep myself looking nice. I stay busy with my job. I thought all I wanted was to be his wife and be happy with him." She swallowed. "I'm not even sure if that's what I want anymore. Or ever wanted."

The woman sucked at her teeth in a loud, rude sound. "He stepping out on you?"

"I really don't know. We don't…I mean—"

"Ain't much heat between you no more?"

A heated blush burned Naomi's neck and chest. She'd never spoken of such things so openly with a stranger. She shook her head.

"Oh, ain't no shame in wanting to screw your own husband. You got a lot of passion in you waitin' to come out."

Naomi stammered again. "I don't really want, um, relations with him all the time. I just want him to, maybe, pay more attention to me. The way he used to when we were younger. He's hardly ever home nowadays." The tears that threatened spilled over onto her cheeks. "I don't want to feel so lonely anymore, especially when he's physically right there. Maybe then we can rekindle the love that isn't so strong between us anymore."

The witch stood in front of Naomi, just an older woman again. "That all you askin' me for?"

Naomi met her gaze, swiping at her eyes. Her voice was strong when she spoke again. "Yes. I want my husband to spend more time with me."

As soon as the words left her mouth, her eyes began to burn from the substance the conjure woman blew into her face. Naomi coughed. She felt nausea starting in her belly. Then, the yearning she'd felt earlier came rushing back, more intense than before. Although her face also stung, she rose and returned to the window closest to her. Movement caught her eye, and she stood, transfixed, wanting to vocalize the longing she felt. She could find no words.

"You best go home to your husband, girl. Go on, now."

When Naomi could turn away from the window, she found the other woman staring at her with slitted eyes.

"Go on, now."

Naomi found herself bundled back into the lift and on the ground below the cabin before she fully comprehended what had happened. Then, the chicken legs unrooted themselves and sprinted through the forest, the house disappearing deep into the foliage.

She didn't have much time to think about the strange happenings in the forest that day because of what manifested at her home.

When she'd walked back toward the house, the first thing Naomi saw was Devon's sports car sitting in their driveway. As she approached, she reached out to feel the hood. Cool to the touch. That meant he hadn't just gotten there in a hurry to beat her home, and had likely been there for a while.

But when she went inside, the house was dead quiet. "Devon…?" She squatted to take off her running shoes, and he appeared in front her bent over form.

"Where have you been?" His typically ebullient, full voice fell flat across the short distance between them.

"I always take my runs at this time during the summer. Keeps me busy." Part of her relished the thought of her husband looking for her and him being the one all alone for a change. The feeling quickly abated when Naomi realized she didn't like being questioned by a virtual stranger.

"I've been waiting for you."

Naomi stood up and tried to walk around him into the kitchen. He shifted to allow her to pass and followed her into the brightly lit room.

She spent the rest of the day trying to walk around him.

While she cooked their lunch, he was right there, standing at her side. When she went to the backyard to water the plants, he joined her. When she tried to go use the bathroom, he went too, and only stayed outside the door when she looked at him pointedly, pressed her hand to his chest, and closed the door in his face. He waited there until she came out and resumed dogging her every step.

The next morning, he hadn't gone in to work. It was sweet to think he had taken the day off to spend time with her. He never did that. In fact, she had a difficult time getting him to stay home from work for any reason, a multitude of accrued personal and sick time, and special occasions be damned.

"What are we going to do today?" She had already decided she'd skip her run that morning since Devon wasn't much into outdoor activities.

"Whatever you want to do." The monotone hadn't left his voice.

"Are you feeling okay? You sound like you might be coming down with something." She stretched out her arm to feel his forehead, and he lay there, allowing her investigation. Not swatting her hand away like he usually did when she doted on him.

"I'm fine." And he continued to lie there in the bed next to her until she got up and began to get dressed. He did the same and followed her out of their bedroom. They spent that first full day in relative silence, him only responding when she asked him something. He never looked at her or started an interaction. And when they went to bed that night, he lay motionless on his side of the bed, staring at the ceiling until she fell asleep watching him.

By the fourth day, Naomi was unbearably uncomfortable with Devon's presence. His movements grew slower, and she often caught a grimace on his face, as if he was in pain.

"I made you a doctor's appointment for today. I don't think you're feeling well."

"Okay."

He followed her to her car and allowed her to drive him into town. She didn't know what to do when the doctor didn't find anything wrong with her husband. Something was way, way off.

"I guess you should go on into work this afternoon," she said, "since the doctor gave you a clean bill of health."

He didn't turn to face her. "Okay. But where will you be?"

"I'll be waiting at home for you like always." She patted his stiff hand with an enthusiasm she didn't feel. When they returned home, she got his briefcase and his car keys and led him to his own car. He got in and drove away.

She headed back into the forest.

There was no sign of the old woman's house where she'd last encountered it. She wandered deeper into the trees, listening and watching for any sign of the chicken legs and the wooden lift.

"You looking for me, girlie?"

Naomi gasped at the voice speaking right in her ear.

"Guessin' that's a yes." The crone stepped out from beneath a distant tree, beckoning Naomi to come to her. Before she could close the distance between them, the wooden lift appeared and tipped her, face front, into it.

"What did you do to him?" She wasn't sure if she was angry or just curious. Then she decided she was a bit of both, curiosity winning out as stronger.

"What did I do to who?" The older woman smirked and pushed her curtains apart to reveal the same desert and ice landscapes Naomi had seen on her first visit.

Instead of answering, she went toward the cold emanating from the glass. Much more detail showed through the pane—Naomi could now make out a little house on the horizon, with smoke coming from the chimney. A tiny figure walked in the snow drift outside the house, deep tracks appearing in its wake as it slowly made its way out into the expanse.

A yearning Naomi only recognized as a deep want started low in her belly. She hadn't felt that magnetism since the last time she'd talked to Devon about having a baby. She'd thought they would have as much time as they wanted to start a family, so when he evaded her talking about it, she took it in stride, determined to bring it up again later.

But soon, later was too late. She was already in her late forties when Devon finally told her he'd never wanted children. The pain of that stabbed through her, and she flinched.

She'd told herself that if it had been meant to be, it would have. Maybe she had been barren. Maybe he had been. Now that she'd started peri-menopause and they rarely had sex, she'd probably never find out.

"I always wanted kids," Naomi spoke the words aloud. She placed her hand on the cool glass in front of her.

"Sometimes what we want ain't necessarily what we need."

"I suppose. That's why I pour my all into my little charges at school." She smiled. "No one stays in the first-grade classroom for more than a couple of years while they establish themselves as teachers. I never wanted to be anywhere else." She thought she had never wanted to be anywhere else, until right then, looking out that window.

The glass grew hot underneath her fingers, and she drew her hand back. The scape changed to the desert, and the light from the sun's reflection heated the glass until it appeared molten. A lone figure trudged through the sand toward a house built into a dune in the far corner of the picture. Despite the heat, Naomi pressed her face against the window, leaning into the pulling sensation.

"What you need?"

Naomi sighed and turned to face the other woman. "I need my husband to want me. To desire me. To not just go through motions you're making him go through. It has to get better if we do it right."

"I knowed you wanted something more. That heat is burning off your ass." She cackled loudly and snorted. "And I ain't making him do nothin'. I did what you said. Just like I'll do what you said now."

Naomi felt the woman's breath on the back of her neck, and her skin began to burn.

She was tired but couldn't quite place the source of her exhaustion. She headed back home to take a nap before Devon arrived home from work.

Naomi woke from her nap to Devon fervently pressing his body onto hers. His intensity caused her to startle, his heat unlike that of the yearning she'd experienced earlier. She tried to lose herself in what was obviously pleasurable for her husband. She missed making love with him.

She just wasn't sure that love was what they were making in that moment. Gone was the ever patient and gentle Devon she'd known. Even when they were in the throes of young passion, he had always been courteous and took his time with her. The man on top of her was anything but courteous.

He rained kisses all over her face and stuck his tongue down her throat. Naomi didn't resist because she wanted to be with him. Just not like that.

"Devon. Baby. Please. Slow down."

He seemed to hear her, but didn't heed her request.

She soon told herself there was no need for him to slow down because her passion had finally caught up to his, and she joined him in their wanton abandonment of propriety, in steamy, satisfying daytime sex.

Devon fell asleep as soon as they finished, leaving Naomi awake. Sated, but unsettled. She'd wanted her husband to desire her, and he had. Surely, at their age, there could only be so much of that—it wasn't like he could physically get on-demand erections all the time, nor could she want to match his desire, even if he could.

Naomi was wrong on all counts. She endured the next three days of non-stop sex until she had a perpetual ache between her legs and bruises on her breasts where Devon grabbed at them.

She woke up the fourth day, determined to tell him she was tired and needed a break. She rolled over to where he lay on their bed and shook his shoulder. A gurgling sound came from his throat, but he didn't move. Naomi raised up to see what was happening. Devon's eyes were bulging open, brown eyes turned cloudy. A heavy trickle of dried blood crusted his jaw. The gurgles turned to a rasp, and Naomi grabbed her cell phone to call 911.

"Devon. Devon! Hang on. They're coming."

She started CPR and tried to distract her mind from the feeling of his cold, hard lips beneath hers, the unyielding flesh beneath her hands preventing her from pressing his chest adequately.

When the EMS arrived, they pulled Naomi away from him and continued her ministrations for a short time before telling her he was gone and had been for hours.

Gone? "What do you mean? We just woke up," she said. "He was trying to tell me something just before you got here."

Naomi tried to focus on what the woman was saying, but she could still hear Devon gurgling, trying to say something. The others didn't seem to hear it.

Then she ran. Out of the house. Into her beloved forest. Straight into the wooden lift.

"What did you do? What did you do to him?" She screamed, anguish ripping across her vocal cords as she twisted her hands together to ground herself in the moment.

"I ain't do nothing but what you asked for." The crone seemed sad, but not repentant.

"I don't...I don't understand. What happened to my husband? What did you do?"

"It was his time to go. I ain't do nothing to speed that along."

Naomi wailed and dropped to the floor. "Did I kill him? Was his heart too weak to have all that sex? Did I do this?"

The other woman wrapped her arms around her and rocked. "No. Was just his time. He was gonna go then anyways, no matter what you had been asking for."

"Why didn't you tell me that? You knew. I could've asked for different things. I could've asked for him to—to stay alive, or to be healed, or...something." She left her biggest thought unspoken—*I could have asked for something I really wanted and needed.*

The witch let go with a melancholy chuckle. She seemed to have heard the thought as clearly as if Naomi had spoken it. "Yep, you shoulda done that. Oh, but you done more than that. You wanted him to spend more time with you and to desire you. That don't stop with death. He gonna keep wantin' you. Always."

Naomi stopped rocking and drew away from the witch. "What do you mean?"

"He gonna keep coming for you, wanting to love on you. That's the power you held and used."

"I don't want him to come for me like that. I want him to rest in peace." Her eyes widened. "You did this. You knew, and you let this happen." She pushed the woman away and clawed at her face.

"Calm down, girlie. Your problem is you don't know what you want or need. I just did what you said." She slapped Naomi. "Now. Think. For real, this time. What you want? What you need?"

Naomi cried, gut-wrenching sobs filling the space in the enormous cabin. "I don't know what I want. I wanted my husband. I thought I needed him."

"Maybe you did. But he gone now, only to return to fill the need you said you had before." She sucked her teeth. "But it ain't gotta be that way."

Icy heat prickled through Naomi, and she crawled across the floor to the expanse of windows, pulling her in.

"You could join me and my sisters. It's only three of us, and we mighty tired. Wanna take a rest. We can't, 'less we find somebody to join us."

Naomi continued toward the far wall of windows. "You did all this to trick me?"

"No tricks. You always got a choice."

When she reached the window, one pane revealed the forest below, where she saw Devon's reanimated corpse shambling through the brush. He sniffed the air, and she knew he could smell her. He would never rest. She would never rest.

That wasn't what she wanted or needed.

She pressed her face fully into the icy section of the window and relished in the blast of cold jolting through her when her body followed. She turned around in the snow and looked at the deep footsteps behind her.

Naomi raised one leg and placed it in the hole in front of her. She repeated the same with the other. Step by step, she marked the progress of the figure before her, back to the cabin, where the horizon kissed the sky.

THREE
REGRETS NEVER DIE

I don't have many regrets, but the ones I do have like to haunt me.

Not because I carry those bastards around with me forever, though, like some kind of Black suffer martyr doll. I don't carry nothing that ain't serving me well. Ain't nobody got time for that shit. Mama always told me to live a life with no regrets, taking everything to the max, and owning your mistakes.

I owned every one of my mistakes and did whatever I had to do to exorcise them from my life and memory. Some memories take longer to die than others. But when I work on it long enough, they still fade away into those recesses of my heart where I have to sometimes wonder if they really ever happened, since they don't hurt no more. There was no way I wanted to relive that shit over and over again. I got other shit to do than grieve forever.

I was still grieving Regret Number Three when that fucker came through the woods surrounding the back of my property and relentlessly banged his head on my bedroom window. Over and over again, he slammed into the windowsill, sloshing, wet connecting sounds. By the time I found a flashlight and got back there, he'd torn new vivid pinkish red slashes into his face, matching the old, oozing, festering ones I'd made deep in his neck and sliced across his chest a few weeks prior when I erased him. Or at least, when I had tried to erase him.

It was 'fore day in the morning, and I ain't have time to deal with him right then. What is this thing haints got with the middle of the night shenanigans?

I figured if I could just put him on hold somewhere for a couple of hours so I could get a little more sleep, I'd just have a bonfire at dawn, the time when us regular folks were up and moving about. I threw on my pajama pants and ran outside with a flashlight, growling at him the whole time to let him know I was none too pleased with his inopportune intrusion.

He tried to reach for me and touch me while I prodded him toward a storage shed with the long handle of the flashlight, his bloated lips puckering up for a kiss I no longer desired. His formerly full, dark lips had grown so decayed they were black, black. Bloated and fuller than they had been in life, when the temptation they'd offered was too much for me to resist.

Maggots slithered across the straight, white teeth he had often shone my way when he wanted something. I had thought they were the prettiest teeth I had ever seen before. Movie star teeth. They weren't so pretty with the rot and bugs...and in the mouth of a nasty man.

I had met him one afternoon while I walked through my woods. I almost shot his ass because he was trespassing.

"No! Please don't shoot!" He'd held up those big, dark, smooth hands and flashed that beautiful smile my way.

I wavered slightly, his voice cutting right through my soul to settle at the bottom of my belly where it did crazy things. I should've known then he'd be trouble because I never hesitated once I raised my shotgun.

"Why not? You on my land, uninvited. The hell you up to?" I lowered my arms and relaxed my stance only a little bit.

"I got lost."

I could tell he was lying. I raised the gun back into position and aimed. "Ain't nothing back here but me and mine. You ain't lost."

"Okay, okay! I didn't get lost." He smiled again, wider, like his life depended on how pretty he could look. It sort of did depend on exactly that. I couldn't blame him for that much effort.

"Ain't gonna ask you again."

"I was looking for you."

The crazy butterflies swam in my belly again at his words. "Why you looking for me?"

"I saw you at the market the other week, and nobody could answer any questions about you. All they'd say was that you lived back here somewhere. I been walking through these trees the past few days, hoping to get lucky and see you." He talked faster and faster till my head started to swim.

"Well, you done found me. Now what?"

I never should've asked that question. He wasted no time in showing and telling me what his intentions were. On the surface, at least. Pretty words from a pretty man. I didn't see the ugliness in his soul until it was way too late.

I gave that man all I had to give and some I didn't know existed. I couldn't deny him anything because I was so glad just to have somebody. It got lonely in them woods, all by myself, all the time. I ain't know I was supposed to hold a little something of myself off from him so he'd wanna stick around. I was basically untried and didn't understand the way shit went between men and women. All I could see and feel was the heat he brought inside me, a feeling I'd never known and one that only elevated once he touched me nicely.

All too soon came the time when his touch wasn't always nice. He was all cuddles and cream while we were in bed. Once outside the bed, not so much. If I so much as turned my head wrong, he went upside it. That's exactly how it happened that first time he hit me.

I lay in the crook of his muscled arm after we'd had sex, and he reclined, smiling like he had just gotten the best gift. He had been a little rough with me, and I hurt deep inside my core, but I figured I'd just deal with it since he looked satisfied. But when he removed his arm from underneath me and sat up on the side of the bed, my jostled body screamed, and I let out a groan. I turned to face him, and he reached around and slapped me, damned hard, filling my face with a pain that rivaled the one down below.

"The fuck you looking at?" He started to get dressed and stood up to leave.

I held my cheek and stared at him from where I still lay, afraid to move again. His eyes didn't match the warmth we had just had between us, and I didn't understand what had changed so suddenly, except that he was no longer in the bed. I thought that might be normal for relationships, though. What did I know? I only had Mama and my father to use as an example, and their fucked up-ness was apparently not the stuff fairy tales were made of.

So I made the best of the time he and I spent in bed. Made myself a good little student. If I knew how to do any damned thing, it was to do exactly what a man told me to do, the way he told me to do it. What I didn't have in experience, I more than made up for with effort and a willingness to learn.

I didn't understand how I knew I might be starting to gain the upper hand in bed at some point, reducing him to a breathless and quivering mass of muscle, acquiescence appearing in his gaze, however fleetingly, before he put his feet on the floor and returned to abusing me again. After the fighting, when we returned to the bed, I resolved to put it on him so good he'd realize he loved me and stop being mean to me forever.

Mama once told me to never give all my good-good to any man because he'd crave that shit till his dying day. Apparently, this one wanted me beyond even his demise. I laughed, a sound more of torment than glee, ringing out in the emptiness and bouncing off the trees before it hit my ears. His ass hadn't wanted me enough not to cheat on me over and over again. He hadn't wanted forever with me when he berated me for imagined slights and pounded his fists into my body over and over again, relentlessly.

He had actually had the nerve to tell me, once he bloodied me up and I was crawling around on the floor in pain, he couldn't even see what he had wanted with me in the first place. When he choked me out and into unconsciousness that last time, I confronted him over his cheating and abuse. I decided I was done with that particular regret.

"You ain't gonna hit me no more."

"Oh, you think so? Imma do what I damn well wanna do. If I wanna kick your ass again, who gonna stop me?" He inched closer to where I had dragged myself up from the kitchen floor, just as I knew he would, unable to resist hovering over me to prepare for one good punch or kick.

I struck first, swiping the large butcher knife across his cheek.

"What the f—?" Before he could grasp what was happening, I lashed out again, slicing the side of his neck. Bright red blood bubbled from the wound, splattering everywhere, commingling with the slower flow falling from his face.

I continued to attack him with the knife, growing stronger each time the metal connected with and separated his skin. I slashed at him even after he stopped trying to fight back and fell to the floor with a heavy thud.

I felt the good memories of lovemaking between us starting to fade with his last breaths. I hoped it wouldn't be too hard to forget him completely. After he was dead, the love should eventually die out, too. Not quite yet, though. I would have to kill that regret again if I wanted the memories to die, too—with fire the next time.

That next morning, I returned to the shack where I had him imprisoned and gave him a few whacks across the head with my sledgehammer to get him to stop trying to subject me to his fake ass dead man lovemaking. He just wouldn't quit! Arms reaching and grasping, and kissy noises with his hanging flesh lips.

Once his head looked like ground hog for making hog-head cheese, I dragged him back off into the forest. The hole he'd climbed out of gaped wide open like my own body had always done for him. That grave was the only hole I should ever have invited his ass into.

After I had gathered all the kindling and set him alight, I sat down a ways away to have my morning coffee. A good fire had always comforted me, as had the movement and smells of the surrounding greenery. Snapping sap from not quite dead branches soothed my nerves with the rhythmic pop, pop, popping sounds. I looked forward to the way the fire teased the moisture out, smoking in sections, until the flames worked their way inside, burning everything.

I loved living in the backwoods of East Texas, where random bonfires were never suspicious. A lack of them was, though, a sure sign your neighbor was a transplant from some other place. Or a crazy person who wasn't altogether right. Not my neighbors. We all assured one another with frequent burnings of various things. I was surrounded by a true native family outside my little patch of 200 acres. I was safe.

Mama taught me not to place my safekeeping into anyone else's hands but my own because she said you can't trust nobody. Not to ever tell anybody your secrets because then they wouldn't be secrets anymore. And once one other somebody knew, you always had to watch them in case they told on you.

I never told anyone anything, until the time I whispered to her that my father had been raping me since I was a little girl. I waited till I was almost full grown to even say that much because I was just tired of a lifetime of pain and stinking breath and pissy man parts jamming into me over and over again, day after day, month after month, year after year. I didn't want that to be a secret no more. I wanted it to be revealed so it wouldn't exist anymore.

I continued my confession, telling her his ass would forever be my first terrible decision, Regret Number One.

"He can't hurt me no more, Mama. I done took care of that."

"What do you mean you took care of that?" Her usually slitted eyes opened wide as she looked at me like she hadn't ever seen me before then.

I held her gaze. "I regret letting him torment me for so long before I did anything about it. But I don't regret what I did to him."

He deserved that hanging and skinning. I rigged up a rope and trapped his ass, flipping him upside down in those same woods I loved, dangling from a tree. I peeled off a slice of his skin for every encounter I could remember him subjecting me to. I ran out of skin and had to start carving chunks out of his muscle and sinew. I ran out of flesh before I could even stop counting my grievances against him.

I scattered the carcass bits throughout the trees, walking all around and throughout the trees, feeding whatever predators wanted to feast on his ass the way he'd eaten at me for years. I returned to his hanging skeleton with bits of clinging flesh, cut him down, and ground the rest of him up in the woodchipper. I fed that reeking slush to the bottom dwellers in the water that lived in the swamp running through my woods.

That regret was gone, gone.

But Mama had become Regret Number Three the night of my confession, and she wasn't gone like I had thought. Five years of peace, and I guess the revival of Regret Number Four shook her loose from her grave. She had slowly started to dig her way up as I watched the bonfire blaze feet away, erasing that man right outta my hair. She came from what I had thought was her forever sleeping spot, a single, mummified hand scraping and clawing at the dirt.

I should have chopped that one up when I cut it off of her.

I'd separated it from her body when she came running at me with the butcher knife the night I finally answered her constant question —a two-week-long song of where her husband had gone—with the truth. A version of it, anyway.

"I ain't asking your ass again. Where is your father?"

"Gone."

"Gone, where?" Her brown eyes blazed with an unrecognizable fury. She had never raised her voice to her husband, and she ignored me most times, unless she was telling me to do something.

That night, the bitch went from the indifferent woman who barely raised me from the margins with full-of-shit sayings into a raging monster set on murder.

"I always knew you wouldn't come to no good, you slut! Prancing around here showing your ass, enticing my husband." She stuck the knife into the old wooden dining table. She pulled it out. Stuck it in again. Harder.

I stood up.

"He couldn't stay away from you. He didn't even look at me no more after you started showing your whore ways."

We circled each other around the table.

"That's why I told him he could have a little taste of you, thinking the shit would get old and he'd stop pining for your ass. But he didn't. The more he got, the more he wanted."

I thought I'd be ready to run when she actually struck out with the knife, but her admission stunned me.

"It was the least your nasty ass could do to help me keep him at home so he wouldn't go running around with the whores in town. We needed to keep him happy here so he would keep. Paying the bills and taking care of me."

She chased me around the table, taking random stabs at me while I tried to get out of the house. I hadn't wanted her to comfort me. That was too much to expect. I also hadn't expected her to admit she knew I was being abused—or try to kill me for real.

"I invited him to dump his perverted lust into your young body so he would keep me a kept woman. Now your ungrateful ass done took away our meal ticket," she said.

That's where she fucked up. She said too much. I stopped running and faced her. She brought the butcher knife down into my leg. I stumbled and wrestled the knife out of her hand.

I straddled her body and stabbed her in the ears, since she hadn't wanted to hear anything I was saying. I cut out her eyes, since she'd turned a blind eye to my suffering all those years. I sliced her tongue in two since she never used it to protect me. When she stopped moving around much, I pushed the knife into her pelvis over and over again, cursing the womb that had given birth to me just to sacrifice me to her demonic ass husband. After she'd taken her last breath, I cut off her hand, just so the bitch would only have one hand in the afterlife to try and flip folks off with.

That one hand was doing a hell of a job right then. I thought I'd seen the last of her corporeal being till she dragged her ass outta that grave. Years dead didn't mean shit when she wanted to fuck with me some more.

I threw my coffee down and ran for my sledgehammer back at the house. That bitch had to be erased forever, with her shitty advice-giving ass. When I got back, I made short work of setting her afire, too. That fire would take forever to burn down with two bodies in the middle of the pile, but I had to reduce them to ash before I could re-bury them. I had to get rid of them for keeps.

After more meditation, I ran back to the house and searched the attic for all the family heirlooms that were made of iron. We were poor, country folks, descended from poor country slaves. We didn't own any silver, or else I would gladly have sacrificed it on those altars of my burning sins. All I had was random bits of iron—mostly cookware and jewelry—to seal in the vault of my own legacy to this world: regrets that won't truly die. I stopped by the yard shed again, taking the sack of rock salt I used to kill weeds with me for extra grave site protection.

That took me the whole day and most of the evening, so I really wasn't ready at all when Regret Number Two came back. I awakened, disoriented, to the sounds of weak mewling from the direction of my bedroom floor. I turned on the bedside lamp and pressed myself against my headboard at the sight, instant pain and tears wracking my body.

I had known better than to try to keep the baby conceived of hate and pain. My only regret toward her was in thinking I deserved to have her, to bring her into our fucked-up family home. I had wanted her so badly, something innocent and pure and all my own. I couldn't stop the sobs as I looked down and watched her tiny body wriggling around on the floor of my bedroom, dried out bones, covered in the reduced-to-rags, small, once beautiful lace dress I had hand sewn to bury her in. She was looking for her mommy.

My own Mama didn't pay enough attention to me to see my middle expanding or my increased appetite. My father seemed disgusted by all the signs, and I'd catch him looking at me sideways often enough. He took less and less interest in me those following months, choosing instead to go into town to visit the whores Mama had tried to keep him away from. He had to know I was with child. The timing of him leaving me alone and my growing pregnancy weren't no coincidence.

Alone and way too young, I gave birth to my baby on the forest floor, surrounded by my beloved trees and the sounds of my own labored breathing. I didn't know exactly how far along I was, but I did know it was really early for the baby to come. When I had managed to expel her from my body, she entered this shitty world with no breath, no sound. No life.

My life seemed over as I cradled her tiny, bloody body and held her tiny hands and feet, counting the fingers and toes, performing the age-old mothering ritual, even though I no longer had a baby to mother. I held her for hours, my daughter and my sister, and wept for the both of us, fatherless girls who ironically shared the same nothing ass father.

I kept her in my bedroom for days, cuddling her and making clothes for her. Mama still hadn't noticed any of that because she was too busy trying to keep my father from going into town after women every night. I had told him I had been on my period for an extended time. He knew I was telling the truth about bleeding because I was still passing afterbirth, and my bloody, soaked pads in the bathroom trash can proved this. As much of a demon as he was, that was one other time he wouldn't fuck with me.

The morning I found maggots squirming around underneath my baby girl's still closed eyelids, and almost hurled at the scent emanating from her tightly wrapped bundling, I noted the bloating of her body, swelling her up and making her look almost like a fully formed baby. I knew then that I had to give her up to her eternal slumber. I dressed her in the prettiest dress I had made and took her out to the woods. I kissed her one last time and lovingly set her into the deep grave I dug for her. The dress was the only thing I had to give her, and I was proud for her to wear it forever.

Only she hadn't worn it in her grave forever. She was right in front of me, returned just like almost all my other regrets. I couldn't stop myself from sliding down to the floor from the side of the bed and picking her up, clumps of dirt clinging to the tattered dress hanging from her skeleton. She sighed in contentment, burrowing deeper into my arms until I could feel her tiny ribs poking at the inner side of my forearms. She didn't really stink that much anymore. It was bearable if I could keep holding her forever.

I tried to remember where I'd put the other clothes I'd made for her those years prior. Mangled thoughts ran through my mind. Our father was long dead, no longer alive as he had been when she was born and buried. My mother wouldn't come back to taint our household with her bullshit anymore. I didn't need to date because that wasn't working out for me, anyway.

I sang to her, and she tilted her eyeless sockets up towards my face. I fell in love with her all over again. This time, I could keep her. I never had to send her away again. She was one regret I didn't mind haunting me forever.

FOUR
THOSE WHO TEACH PAY KNOWLEDGE FORWARD

Georgia stared at the empty desk where her student, Calvin, should have been sitting. He had missed a lot of class recently. She scanned the room to see if she could pinpoint another student she might be able to ask about him. Her gaze met that of the youngest child in the room. The girl wore an elaborate tunic and fidgeted with the hem of the garment with one hand while twirling her long braid with the other. She stared wordlessly at Georgia. Georgia smiled. The girl did not smile back.

Calvin did not have any friends or neighbors who lived close to him, only social acquaintances she saw him interact with superficially during recess and class activities. He probably would not have been friends with the little girl who was far too young to engage with him. Her concern for Calvin deepened at the realization that he was as solitary as the young child who walked out of the room, into the bright Texas sun.

Most of the children in her small, one-room schoolhouse had quite a few obstacles to overcome in getting their education. Some came from families who did not see the value in an education beyond being able to count money and plan crops. Others had to complete chores on their homesteads before they could attend the classes. Some of the older children had jobs throughout town, and only through her incessant pleas since she had arrived there three years prior had the business owners been persuaded to allow the young people to attend class for at least a couple of hours each weekday.

For those students who did not have job duties preventing them from attendance, other financial circumstances often came into play. The vast majority of the families in the town and its surrounding areas were of meager means. Through her conversations with parents, she quickly realized many of the children would be allowed to attend classes only so they could take two of their daily meals at the schoolhouse. The same importunities she had directed towards the wealthier citizens to maintain student attendance had also yielded food and firewood donations for her to feed them.

Resources would always be an issue, especially when depending on the generosity of fellow humans. For now, Georgia was able to provide warmth, meals, and all the knowledge she had to share with her pupils. The country was on the precipice of being a grand nation, and she wanted her students to be educated as she had been, to go on to college, and then do the best they could to gain visibility in the nation that had not always afforded such to most people of color.

Calvin was a bright kid who submitted all his assignments. Georgia worried he would fall behind in their coursework when he neglected to physically attend school as frequently as he had taken to doing. She could only send the work to his grandparents' home so many times before the gaps in his education would start to show due to his missing the organic discussions and impromptu alternative journeys they often took in the classroom.

She understood he had lived with his grandparents on the outskirts of town since he was an infant, his mother having passed away during one of Texas's rare harsh winters years ago. She had only had the chance to chat with the two elders on a few occasions, and it was clear they cared for Calvin and wanted him to get an education. However, they no longer farmed their land, having leased out the farming rights to another family in return for a slim but steady income and food provisions in their later years.

Calvin had no interest in farming, anyway. He had expressed this sentiment to his classmates and Georgia on numerous occasions. He wanted no parts of bartending, blacksmithing, horse tending, or construction—most of the occupations available to young Black men in their part of the country. Calvin wanted to be a doctor. To do that, he had to graduate from school and apply to, then attend, college.

Georgia often shared what information she gleaned about medical school training in the US and abroad with the boy. Although a Black physician had recently graduated from Dartmouth College, Calvin could not rely on any fleeting benevolence from the admissions board to guarantee him admittance. He would likely need to attend medical school in Europe.

She felt in her spirit that working as a healer was Calvin's calling. He was smart enough to meet the educational requirements and compassionate enough to care for his patients. She would do whatever she needed to make sure he got into college. What was required of her in that moment was checking on Calvin and his grandparents.

She saw her students as more than just bodies to be talked at and reasons for her to keep a job. Georgia very much cared about actually helping them to learn all they could about the world they lived in, especially their still-developing country. She had spent her childhood in Ohio, wishing to get away from the stench and overcrowding of her rapidly growing town. When she graduated from Oberlin College, her only desire was to head out west and find a rural community that needed a teacher.

Georgia Watkins had ended up in Texas, where she would live out her remaining days. And her deepest desire was that the students she taught would do the same as she had, answering a heartfelt call to go back and help other community members to build lives of joy and accomplishment. Others would escape to different parts of the world to thrive in productive lives. Georgia smiled when she thought of her part in the whole educational cycle.

Her expression turned contemplative when she returned her thoughts to Calvin. Yes, there was something very special about the boy, besides his personhood and how quickly he picked up on anything he wanted to learn. She did not know exactly what it was, though she had her suspicions. She only knew she had to talk to him and persuade him to return to school.

Georgia stepped gingerly through the fallen corn stalks that covered the gradually disappearing trail. She had worn her most serviceable boots to protect her feet. The Johnsons' homestead lay beyond the well-worn path leading out of town in that direction. She would have to travel through high grass in some places, and while she was unafraid to do so, she did not want the basket she carried to tumble from her arms. The school's leftover yeast rolls, sliced ham, and fresh carrots she carried as an offering to the Johnsons would likely go a long way towards helping out, even if the family saved the food for the next day.

She waved at the two older gentlemen walking through the distant remnants of the cotton harvest on the other side of the field. Neither waved back, although they both stood from their bent positions to watch her as she passed them. The fields were not pretty in the aftermath of the harvest season, but Georgia loved the smell of worked land, having given its life-sustaining produce as it slowly returned to the ground from which it grew, to make the soil richer for the next harvest.

Where outsiders to their rural community saw desolation and poverty, she saw less gluttonous hoarding of wealth and a community that provided for its members in ways those outsiders rarely understood. This farming community of theirs wanted everyone to have a fighting chance to make it through the hard times plaguing them all.

A woman dressed in a serviceable calico dress and bonnet held the hand of a small boy as they fell into step a good distance away from Georgia. Their feet fell without sound on the grass. Georgia nodded her head in greeting. The two looked in her direction and continued along their journey without disturbing her pace. She smiled at the dogs chasing each other ahead of her.

She stopped for a second, in overwhelmed exhilaration, surrounded by life and death and everything in between. People outside their little town seemed to forget they lived whole life cycles in the rural communities, just as those who lived in the larger towns did. Folks were born, made the best life they could, and died, just the same as their human brethren across the world. The interactions between the living and the dead existed in beauteous wonderment that never ceased to amaze Georgia.

That was one of the main reasons Georgia went to visit Calvin and his grandparents: she wanted him to have a chance to thrive and go on to college and have a fighting chance at building a life he wanted to live, continue his own life cycle while helping others through theirs. She set out to do whatever she could to aid Calvin and his family in making it through any obstacles they were facing.

The schoolwork and meeting the learning objectives were not Calvin's obstacles. She had created an advanced, individualized curriculum just for him when he had devoured the lessons she gave to the other students. He was thin and sometimes dozed off in class, but many teenage boys were thin and did not get enough sleep at home. She suspected the family could likely use extra food every now and then, so they could eat well and so Calvin could get more adequate sleep. She made a note to reach out to a few merchants in town to see if they could help out with extra provisions for the Johnsons if it came to that.

Georgia had just felt the beginnings of sweat rivulets running down the middle of her back when she finally arrived at the modest Johnson home. As she knocked on the heavy wooden door, she scanned the fields surrounding the home, taking note of the beautiful mature trees dotting the land. She also noticed the few other people walking in the general vicinity, none of whom were the Johnsons. There were no other homes close by.

After a respectable amount of time passed from her first, unanswered knock, Georgia knocked again. She shifted her weight from one foot to the other and peered unobtrusively through a small gap in the faded muslin drapes on the dusty front window. An elderly woman sat upright, motionless, on the edge of a beautifully worked, detailed wooden bench. Her wrinkled hands rested on her thighs. She never looked in the direction of the front door or window. Georgia raised her hand to knock again when the door creaked open, and Calvin's face appeared in the crack.

"Ms. Watkins?" His surprised question held a hint of something else. Fear.

"Hi, Calvin. I came to check on you."

He lowered his eyes and mumbled. "I'm fine. You ain't...you didn't have to come all this way."

"Oh, but I did. When the Sun told me you might have been kidnapped by Hades, I had to come in search of one of my top students."

The boy smiled through the crack in the door. "I haven't been kidnapped. If I had, I wouldn't eat any old seeds."

"That's a relief. Then I and your classmates will not have to split time with you here and in the underworld." She moved the basket to her other arm. "We've missed you in class."

He lowered his gaze again. "I have to take care of things here." He made no move to open the door further.

"I understand. But how will you ever go to college if you miss so much school? There are communities around the world that will desperately need the medical training you must get." Georgia could see Calvin weighing her words.

"Remember how we talked in class about paying knowledge forward? About helping our people. Teaching—leading?"

She lowered her voice so only he could hear. "I was hoping I could talk to you and your grandparents about your absences." She then raised her voice back to a regular level. "You aren't in trouble. You're a brilliant student, and I just want to make sure you all have everything you need."

The fear she'd originally seen in trace amounts moments ago came through heavily on the teenager's face.

"MeeMaw and Pops ain't really up for company right now," he mumbled.

Georgia placed her hand on top of his, where he gripped the door underneath the wooden plank lock.

"It's okay. I won't stay long. I really need to talk to you all."

Calvin continued to stare at a point below him. Finally, he mumbled again.

"Just give me a couple of minutes. You can sit in here while I go get them from the back room." He opened the door slowly and ushered her into a dark front room.

Georgia nodded in greeting toward where the old woman sat, while allowing her eyes to adjust to the darkness.

The small, overcrowded room looked pretty much like most of the others in their community, excepting the homes of the wealthier townsfolk. Large, expertly crafted wooden furniture scattered throughout the space, almost—but not quite—too large for the small area. Bric-a-brac filled every available surface and corner, odds and ends from lives of material scarcity and emotional wealth. An ornate wooden cross hung above the open fireplace, where a low flame burned to take the chill from old bones.

One group portrait hung on another wall. She could not make out the individual faces in the picture, but she could feel the pride emanating from the figures, vague outlines commemorating family history. Sacrifices made to purchase the luxury of a new innovation.

The lingering odor of pork neck bones wafted through the air, and Georgia's stomach grumbled. Her eyes began to water, and she swallowed down the growing lump in her throat. She missed her mother. She missed the loving comfort of her childhood home, which often smelled of various cheap cuts of meat, seasoned and cooked so well they tasted better than more expensive food she got elsewhere. Food was love, all across the diaspora. The positive energy in the home helped assuage her worry about Calvin: his grandparents' house was full of love.

Georgia finally heard shuffling from a hallway, and Calvin slowly walked back into the room, flanked by his grandparents. Both elderly people walked slowly, Calvin guiding them towards the bench. His grandfather stared straight ahead, following Calvin's murmured direction. Stiffly, he sat down first. Calvin's grandmother took a few extra, guided steps to a point farther on the bench, then sat where Georgia first saw her sitting through the window, and when she had entered the room. Calvin sat between them in the tiny space left between the two.

Georgia cleared her throat. "I'm sorry to bother you, Mr. and Mrs. Johnson. Thank you for giving me a little bit of your time this evening." The Johnson family remained silent, the elderly members not looking directly at her but somehow *through* her. Neither of them accepted her greeting or asked if Calvin was in trouble.

"Calvin is a wonderful student, and I enjoy having him in class."

"Thank. You." The two words uttered by Mr. Johnson sounded like two different sentences, slow and raspy. His voice held the remnants of a robust tone now gone flat.

"I'm concerned about his absences. He mostly keeps up with the assignments, but he misses a lot of the material we cover in class. I'm sure Calvin has discussed his plans for college with you, and if he is to attend in the next year, we have to get him back in class."

"Our Calvin is a good boy." Mrs. Johnson's voice hissed into the room.

"He is a good boy." Georgia's gaze lingered on Calvin, sitting quietly between his grandparents. In the dim light, she could see a light sheen of sweat starting to cover his forehead.

"I just wanted to check in with you to see if there was anything you needed to help get Calvin back to school regularly."

"Thank. You." Mr. Johnson repeated.

Calvin wrinkled his eyebrows into a frown. His breath came in shallow bursts. The older man opened his mouth and closed it again and again several times, like a fish gasping to breathe air outside the water. Georgia continued to watch, her focus shifting to Calvin.

Mrs. Johnson moved her lips again. "Our Calvin is a good boy."

Georgia held Calvin's gaze for long moments before she replied.

"Yes, Ma'am." She stood up. "I can see that Calvin is well cared for, and you have a beautiful home. I know you both will do whatever we must to keep him on track to graduate next year. You all have a good night."

When she got to the door, she asked, "Calvin, after you get your grandparents settled again, could you please come for a short walk with me?"

The boy wiped his still glistening face with the back of his forearm. "Yes, Ma'am."

Georgia stepped off the porch and waited for him, watching a mid-sized black bird sitting motionless on a low branch in the large tree in Calvin's yard. When the boy joined her, she waved him over to the tree.

"See that bird there?" She pointed to the branch.

He squinted. "What bird?"

"Focus your eyes on that other tree across the field. Then pay attention to what shows in your peripheral gaze." Georgia guided Calvin so he fully faced the focal tree, with the closer tree to the side of him.

He did as she instructed. After several moments, his eyes opened wider. Then, he turned his head back to the tree, to the house, to the tree again. "There *is* a bird there! Why can't I see it straight on?"

"I'll have to help you train yourself to see that way." Georgia ran her foot softly through the grass underneath the tree. She picked up a feathered carcass that lay there.

She took her free hand and alternated between making a circle around the body and a sweeping motion towards the branch until the feathered wings began to flutter weakly. The bird opened its eyes but made no effort to leave her hand.

"Ms. Watkins…how?" Calvin reached out and touched the bird. He suddenly dropped his hand and glanced at the branch. Tears filled his eyes.

"You know what I was doing with MeeMaw and Pops." He spoke quietly.

"I do."

"Please don't tell. I'm not doing anything bad. Am I? I don't have anywhere else to go, and I gotta stay in school and graduate."

"I won't tell."

Calvin visibly relaxed, only to suddenly tense up again. "You can do it, too."

"Yes. I can do a lot more." Georgia waved her hand over the bird's body, and the feathers stopped moving. The creature's soul returned to the branch. She gently lowered the corpse back onto the ground.

"The souls of the dead stick around for a bit after their bodies die. They don't really know what else to do, sometimes." She began to walk out towards the field surrounding Calvin's house. He fell into step next to her.

"If the body remains close, people like us can place the souls back inside and keep the body reasonably functional."

Calvin nodded. "Yes. I figured that out with my grandparents. They got sick and then passed away two days later. I didn't know what to do. They didn't want me to go get Doc to come out, and I had no one else to help. I didn't want to leave them. They died. I couldn't help them." He ended on a swallowed sob and took deep, shuddering breaths.

"I begged them not to leave me, and they opened their eyes again. But I couldn't see them when I would lay them down." He swiped at the tears on his face.

"I saw your grandmother sitting in the front room before you let me in. I suspect your grandfather is also around. Their spirits haven't left the house. Now they wait for you to need them and help them back inside their bodies. As long as you have their bodies, they'll stay."

"How—how long can they exist this way?"

"It depends. If you feed their bodies a little bit and let their spirits back inside them every now and again, they'll last a good while. At least for the year, you need to finish school and get ready to go to college." She placed her hand on his shoulder to force him to look at her.

"But you don't want to keep them like that for any longer than you must. They aren't at rest like this. At some point, you have to release them so they can find peace."

Tears welled up in his eyes again. "I don't know how to live without them."

"You may not have to live without their spirits. See those men in the field there?" She pointed to the men she had passed earlier. "And that lady with the little boy?"

Calvin took a few moments to focus, then nodded.

"You learn so quickly! They stay because their bodies are long buried, but they found some type of peace here. After their bodies are buried, your grandparents may decide to remain here, around the loving home you all have."

The boy nodded. "Will they worry about me? Will they be sad?"

She raised her arm to run her hand over the kinky curls on top of his head. "They'll always worry about you, as parents do. But they won't be sad. They have each other. And they'll always be proud of you, going out into the world to find your destiny."

They stood in the field for a few minutes longer. Calvin nodded again.

"They'll be fine when you're not here. We'll start telling the townspeople that they've mostly taken to their bed so folks won't try to disturb them. I expect to see you in class tomorrow."

"Yes, Ma'am."

"Make sure you eat the food I brought so it doesn't go to waste."

"Yes, Ma'am."

"Good evening, Calvin. Everything will be fine."

The next morning, Georgia stood outside the door of the schoolhouse to greet her students with biscuits and milk for breakfast. The little girl in the tunic stood next to her. Georgia caught sight of Calvin in the distance, hands in his pockets, a mid-sized dog lumbering slowly next to him. As they drew closer, she could see that the dog had one eye and moved in an odd way that only she would notice. She smiled widely at the boy.

"Good morning, Calvin. I see you have a new friend. He's welcome to stay out here to wait for you."

He grinned back. "Yes. This is Chester." He waved to the little girl. She waved in return and followed him inside the classroom.

"Well, okay then." Georgia shook her head and chuckled, following them. "Make that *two* new friends."

FIVE

THE BADLY TERRIBLE, ABSOLUTE WORST

E verybody has seen that horror movie. You know the one. It's the sole reason no one drives behind trucks carrying certain kinds of loads.

That movie is the main reason why I stayed to the back side-corner of the shiny red pick-up truck that seemed better suited for a car show than for the actual hauling of stuff. Well, that and the fact I simply couldn't stand to hear my husband grumble about any more damages to my car. He'd just gotten it from the body shop, and I was doing my best to avoid all flying rocks, critters, and imagined obstacles that might even consider hitting my car or jumping in the road.

I just couldn't stand to hear him fuss at me anymore about things I couldn't completely control. Grumble, grumble, grumble. That's all he did these days. Any sparse conversations we used to have had devolved into him yelling at me and me pretending it didn't hurt that I was afraid to do anything in my own house, with my own stuff.

It was bad.

I sipped my morning coffee, not wanting to travel down that road of unhappiness. A rising giggle helped keep me from ruminating on the state of my marriage when I noticed the heavy metal appliances in the back of the truck starting to move around. The giggle escaped when I imagined the tantrum that would result from the damage the rusted, old-timey ice boxes would do to the truck bed. They would scratch the heck out of that piece, even if there was a fancy truck liner. The owner deserved that for not knowing how to pick a real work truck for work.

My chuckle escalated into a full-bodied cackle as the ends of the heavy chains that were wrapped around the fridges clanked against the exterior of the truck, resounding with a bang I could hear even over the drone of the morning news. That pretty little plaything was gonna be banged up real good when the trip was over.

Stewing over someone else's imagined bad luck while I escaped my hellhole of a home to an equally crappy job that was sucking the rest of my soul out was the height of pettiness. I just needed to spread some of the shit around a little, you know?

The hilarity of it all stuck in my throat, my heart, and my breath, when one of the heavy chains in the back of the truck impossibly snapped, whipping away down the highway pavement, sending tiny sparks along the concrete where it struck.

The first fridge followed into the busy traffic. I spun my car out of the way just in time to see the second iron beast leap off the back of the truck with a nimbleness that was quite impressive, even when the terrifying realization that it was coming straight for me registered.

I couldn't avoid the acrobatics and remained transfixed on the box as it smashed into the windshield before I could close my eyes. The only sensation I was aware of was the burning shards of ice cutting, slicing, shredding the tissue behind my eyelids. The slicing intensified as the car rotated and flipped. Down, down.

It was terrible.

I hadn't counted how many revolutions the car made before I passed out, but I guessed I must have gone over the railing at the deep ravine underneath the beltway along the more rural side of the route. That meant the car had travelled quite a ways down, as that was the deepest part of the route along the roadway.

I shivered, giddy. I could feel cold on parts of my arms, one of which hung down to my right side, into the small open space in the part of the car dome that wasn't smashed in. However, I couldn't feel my legs. Trying to open my eyes created a new burning accompanied by a slow trickle of thick liquid dripping down my cheek.

My mind raced. I hung upside down, but sideways. Much of my body was numb, but the seatbelt cutting into part of my neck kept me focused. I tried to move one arm and was met with jagged metal surrounding me. And more dripping liquid.

I hoped the liquid wasn't Freon. The sickly-sweet odor that accompanied many childhood adventures in the old neighborhood, poking at old refrigerators, didn't appear. Relief never took hold, though.

My concern about the quickly cooling substance changed. I heard a sucking sound. Wet and plodding. Quiet and slow at first, then quickening. I was so cold. I could be imagining things. Maybe I was dying.

Surprisingly, that wasn't altogether the worst thing.

Worse than that was the chewing. At first, I was giddy with excitement that I could move some bits of my body. I stopped trying to move when the first bite seared through my arm. Biting, gnawing. Burrowing. On my hands. Through my forearms. Moving down through my shoulders with a "pop" as something escaped my skin and latched onto my cheek.

I ventured another attempt at opening my eyes, and only the one next to the latched thing complied. Blurry, wet motion slid down my cheek, towards my still heavy, opposite eye. Smaller movements behind my lid ramped up, faster and faster, toward the opening.

The thing in my car with me was still sliding from out of the refrigerator, lodged in my hood and windshield. Its body undulated through the crevice created between the meeting of the metal objects until it was fully upon me. The movements met from inside my body and out.

This. This was the absolute worst thing: knowing I would feel enough of myself being made into a meal that I wouldn't be able to even die peacefully.

THE DARKEST ANGEL

"I don't think I'll grow up, so I don't want to be anything."

Ebony's job was necessarily harsh, though never as heartbreaking as hearing those ominous words coming from the mouth of the babe before her. Monarch was only four years old, and he would grow up to be a critical player in the global business stage. For his family, The Family, and all of humanity. He was why Ebony had been placed within The Family. She was tasked with ensuring he lived to grow up, fully protected.

She drew him in for a hug, intoxicated by the innocence of his spirit, surprised again at how welcoming The Royale Family had been to her. It helped that Emperor found her current form pleasing. Wide eyes, thick hair, and a bright, dimpled smile went a long way toward gaining favor with humans. Even Monarch's birth mother, Teena, whom Ebony had been fully prepared to work around and fight at every turn, instead embraced the new woman in her ex-lover's life as a stable and positive influence for their son.

Ebony wasn't always liked, but being so on that assignment helped her cement herself into the boy's life for this situation.

"Why would you say that, sweetie?" Of course, you'll grow up to be strong and powerful." Ebony stroked the boy's long braids, vowing to redo them again once the battle was over.

He stared at her. His guileless, open gaze seeing deeply into her. "Daddy says we have to be about that life and defend family to the end. I can't be scared to die." He lowered his eyes. "And I can't walk around with my mind full of fairy tales and make-believe stuff. Gotta keep it real."

The last of his statement held the secret they shared between the two of them. Monarch had tried to tell his parents about their beloved new family member's alternate identity, but they heard none of it. Ebony had assured the boy it was okay for them to be the only two to know.

Teena entered the room and sat on the couch across from them. "That's right. No fairy tales here. My baby knows family comes first. He's ready for whatever, just like the rest of us. Ride or die."

Ebony trained her large, gentle smile on Teena and spoke without anger. "Why would you put that on this baby? He will have a long and prosperous life. Nations will bow to him and hold him in the highest of reverence." She punctuated her proclamation with a kiss atop his head. He gave her a tight smile and ran over to his mother to show her the worksheet about careers he and Ebony had just completed.

Teena's eyes misted as Monarch climbed into her lap. "I used to pray it could be so. I...we...would die for him, to give him any future beyond the one waiting for him."

Ebony nodded. "Yes, we all would protect him with our lives." Only some of them would die in that effort, and though Ebony could not share that she would not be included in that immediate number, she hoped the other woman found some solace in her words.

"Here are my favorite people." Emperor's heavy voice resonated through the large room before he entered. The tall, dark, muscled man was used to being the center of attention, and Ebony watched how those around him willingly acquiesced. He strode over to where she sat, his nimble silence belying his size and the strength of his presence, followed by several of his closest generals.

She leaned into his kiss. "I've missed you," he murmured.

Ebony smiled and placed her small hands on both sides of his face. "You were understandably busy building and protecting your empire, my Emperor."

"Our empire, baby." His second kiss held genuine affection. Ebony felt his hesitation to pull away from her to greet his son and Teena.

The compound home situation with large, connected living spaces worked best with everyone in The Royale Family under the same set of roofs. The generals were in close proximity for battle and planning, and Ebony, Teena, and Monarch were best protected there.

Emperor and the generals gathered around the bar in the second seating area in the far corner of the room. Ebony clearly heard their conversation, though they took care to speak in lowered tones.

"Word on the street is they're gonna hit us soon. Likely within the week."

"We're ready. Everybody will stay close to home so we can take care of them real quick."

"Bet."

"Cool."

"Alright."

Their planning devolved into light-hearted ribbing and discussion of sports.

Ebony looked up when Jericho, one of the youngest generals, approached Emperor and whispered something to him.

The larger man waved his hand, and Jericho returned to the foyer to lead a group of men inside the room. Marco Ruggiero recognized her, and his eyes widened. He understood that, if she was on a job, many people would die. He had no way of knowing whether his number was up, and it shook him.

Ebony shook her head, almost imperceptibly, at him. His day was coming, but not that day. The Big Boss still needed him in Intake. She was working Outtakes alone on that one. She wanted to laugh at his fear. He was going to cause all the deaths to be seen on that day. There was no room for her to contribute.

Emperor stood and embraced the newcomer. "Zio. What brings you out today?" He seemed happy to see the older man, but unannounced home visits were naturally under deep suspicion, even among close members of The Family.

Marco pointed to a still steaming dish one of his men held. "Marie got to cooking, and you know she can never cook just a little bit."

"Ah. Monarch loves Zia's cooking. Please send her our regards."

Marco clapped Emperor on the back and sat in a chair at the counter. All the generals followed suit.

"You know I hate to drop in without notice. At least I didn't come with my hands swinging, eh?"

"It's never a problem for you to stop by. You're my uncle, closer than blood. You always took care of my Pops, and for that, I'll always take care of you."

"Me and your Pops? Forget about it. He had my back closer than anybody else ever did. God rest his soul." Marco crossed himself and bowed his head in momentary reverence.

After a brief silence, he spoke again. "Word on the street is you wanna ease up on the weight you're pushing out here. Pass it to another arm of The Family." He pulled a cigar out of his shirt pocket and tilted it toward Emperor. "Smoke?"

Emperor declined and hit a small switch in the counter that turned on the silent fan to pull the cigar smoke upwards.

"Yeah. Monarch is getting big. I wanna expand my household with Ebony. Cuff her, you know. Live a little quieter. I finished my master's, and I can go legit on some stuff."

Marco puffed and nodded, blinking at the mention of the declarations for Ebony's eternal affections. His disgust didn't offend her. She didn't exist to experience love or happiness, though she sometimes got wisps of both while working.

"We'll stay with the bud, because that shit's about to hit legal anyway. But the guns and pills, that's too much." He glanced over to where his son stood with the women in his life. "I just wanna simplify things."

One of Marco's generals stood up and gestured to his crotch. The men laughed as he stood and walked back to the foyer. Light ribbing followed him for his "old bladder."

Marco nodded again. "So, what do we do about all the business you'll be leaving on the floor? Nobody else will be able to get the hold in these 'hoods that you have. Your father built those bonds, and they're strong. Can't just give all that up. The Family Caspana is just waiting for us to slip up to take some of our territory."

Emperor ran his hand over his head. "I don't think of it as giving it up. The Caspanas will stay on their sides of town if we empower my people here." He leaned toward Marco. "Listen, Zio. The world is changing. My people are trying to move beyond addiction and dependence. The pills ain't moving like they used to. People are getting jobs and keeping them. Looking to do something beyond… this." He held the older man's gaze. "I want to move beyond this bondage. We don't need more addicts or hunger or poverty. We need progress and prosperity. We won't find that in these drugs and violence."

Marco stubbed his cigar out in the ashtray and stared at Emperor for a long moment. A smile broke across his face, not quite reaching the grayed sideburns along his cheeks.

"I got you. No problem. You're still Family, always. We'll figure it out."

The two men continued to chat about various things. The conversation inside Marco's head wasn't as light and frivolous.

You gotta forgive me, Freddie, my man. I know this is your boy. He's Family. I made promises to you, my dearly departed brother. But he's dangerous to all of us now, with his talk of progress and prosperity and going legal. We can't trust him to stay loyal.

If there was any other way, I'd take it. This will break my Maria's heart. She won't ever know I was behind it, but I feel like shit for the hurt coming her way.

The little man would've made a good leader for The Family if his Pops hadn't gone soft. I'll make sure they're all put away real nice. And I'll make a fat donation to the Baptist church in their names.

Ebony could hear the general who went deeper into the house on his mission, finishing up. A different man had placed cameras throughout the compound weeks earlier on a scheduled visit. Ebony knew where all the cameras were, though she wouldn't show up on any of them. Marco's men watched and waited until the best time to make the strike. The last part was to place explosives that night, and then it would be show time.

After a while, Marco stood and hugged Emperor, an extra-long embrace whose strength permeated through the room. Ebony could see the sheen of tears in his eyes. He bowed to the women. "Ladies. Have a good night."

The household settled in for the evening, Monarch cuddling up with Teena, the men speaking in lowered tones underneath the muted light. Emperor dismissed them and joined Ebony on the couch.

"That wasn't as bad as I thought it would be. Glad it's over, though."

"He was okay with your plans?" Ebony knew the answer. She was surprised Emperor got it wrong.

"I think he was. He knows things have to change sometimes. I ain't separating from The Family. Just breaking off a little bit. Building something strong and more positive for Monarch and for us." He rubbed her stomach, and she relished the human sensations flowing through his fingertips.

"Don't you ever think about us continuing to build? Giving Monarch some sisters and brothers? Us settling down, maybe travelling some?" He lay his head on her shoulder and whispered.

"I've hardly been outside Texas my whole life. I wanna see Europe. Maybe buy a couple of houses across the pond. Have my babies learn other languages."

Ebony remained silent. She would never darken his dream by telling him things were as bleak in Europe as they were in Texas—across every place and time. The whole world was dying, ravaged by dark wills and darker money. He would never see the brighter day he wanted for his children.

But Monarch would. He would reign supreme with the bloodline from The Royale Family and Ebony's protection and tutelage. The Big Boss trusted only her for that all-important task. Yes, the world was in ruin, but it would be built back up, for Monarch to rule illimitably over all.

Emperor rubbed his eyes, tired, and returned to the counter to look over some paperwork.

Ebony did not have to hear the moment she knew was coming.

Emperor suddenly leapt from his stool and ran to stand beneath an innocuous spot on the ceiling, underneath a large ivy plant. "What the…? Generals! Go!"

The generals in the room followed his command, firearms appearing from holsters and hidden spaces around the room. Cameras shattered beneath bullets, but not quickly enough for the men's positions to be determined.

The wet sound of body-muffled gunshots rang through the doorway. Ebony tucked Monarch into her arms and ran toward the hidden entryway they'd trained around in drills. She pressed the entry keys and waited for Teena to join them.

She knew she wouldn't. Teena brandished her own weapon and sprayed the doorway with ammo just as the first of their attackers breached it. She held the line with Emperor and the generals. "Y'all go in!" she yelled.

Ebony's wings emerged from the human skin covering them, and she used small, fallen pieces to fashion earplugs for Monarch. She wrapped him into her feathered embrace and held him fast with her scaled, second set of long appendages. She took great care to refrain from scratching him with her talons as she eased him into an opening pouch underneath her chest.

At first, only Emperor saw her, his momentary distraction earning him a bullet to the neck. Still, he stood, shooting body after body on his way down to the floor. One by one, the generals fell, their pools of blood and body matter mixing with that of their opponents. Teena gazed directly at her, holding the non-fatal wound in her stomach.

"Take care of our baby," she murmured.

Ebony made sure Monarch could not see his parents, keeping him cocooned within her pouch. She knelt beside Emperor, who unsuccessfully tried to reach out to her. She lay a feathered hand to his forehead and pressed her human-like lips to his. He was a good person who had done bad things, but wanted the best for his people.

She couldn't pass judgment on whether or not he deserved the fate their opps had bestowed on him. She only understood that his time had come, and it had to be. There was nothing she could do except make the passing as comfortable as she could, without interfering in the outcome. Ebony entered his thoughts, penetrating the panic stealing across him as he realized he was dying. She showed him Marco's moment of death first, closer than any of them knew. She then passed him fast images of Monarch growing up, training, and taking charge of his destiny. Ruling the world. Becoming the man his father wanted him to be.

Then she sucked and suckled until she felt his life essence fill her. His hopefulness exhilarated her, his ultimate despair choking her. She waited until his sadness was replaced with acceptance and the ecstasy of release before pulling away from his body and walking over to Teena.

The other woman had an even more terrifying blueprint for the end of her life. Her painful wound would not cause her death, but the gang of men who would come through the door next would rape and torture her before they gave her any mercy of death as respite. At the end, she would die in agony. Ebony stroked her face, not wanting that for her.

"Protect our baby," Teena whispered again.

Ebony nodded and pressed her lips to Teena's, again relishing in the high that came with devouring the soul of another who gave it willingly. She allowed images of Monarch growing strong, starting his own family, turning old with them surrounding him to fill his mother's consciousness. Teena smiled, acquiescing and giving her soul to the one who would make sure her baby lived a good life.

Ebony stood for a moment, packaging the two spirits inside her being to share with Monarch later, after they got to safety. His parents had killed people and engaged in shady business, selling drugs and providing guns that perpetuated violence through their neighborhoods. But they had only followed what they knew. Monarch's parents had done the right things in the end, at the moment of their deaths, and their spirits would help make Monarch strong. Resilient. For as long as Ebony had lived among humans throughout her long life, she could never manifest the human spirit of love and strength, and the powerful will of knowledge gained and authentic repentance.

Monarch would be fed completely by them.

At the moment of their impending deaths, the other people in the fracas could see Ebony's true form, but she was not worried they would reveal her. Only the certainty of demise brought the revelation, meaning none of them would live to tell her tales. She strode through the flesh and blood that covered what used to be her temporary home, soothing Monarch, where he remained balled up against her body. His breathing was rhythmic, as her rolling gait lulled him further into sleep. It was easier that way, for him to awaken to his new life with no memory of the details about how it came to be.

Ebony crashed through the far wall of the building and leaped into the darkness surrounding the fallen compound. Flickers of flames from the other side lit the way before her as she headed up across trees with her precious package. She took flight, buoyed higher by the combination of her own strength and that of the two unexpected means of continued support and protection for her ward.

She would keep his body healthy and protected. She would teach him warfare and make sure he gained a perfect education. He would learn at the feet of the gods and great humans before him, taking lessons from their defeats and replicating their triumphs. The essence of his parents would be his capstone: He would be the one true king, their Monarch, ruling illimitably over all.

SEVEN
GRAND OPENING

The thing Althea most loved about being one of the first people on campus every morning was the solitude—no one was there besides her and a couple of the early morning shift safety officers whom she very rarely ran into. The halls smelled of coffee as the café brewed its liquid lifeline for the throngs of students and staff who would come rushing in another couple of hours. She never even saw the café workers, only knew they were there by the smells of breakfast.

This is why she halted when she got off the elevator on her floor, freezing in the cool foyer that had yet to be heated by too many bodies in its space. The hallway led to her office, tucked away in plain sight. A slim figure stood at the other end, holding a large bouquet of balloons. She wasn't sure what was more startling—the fact that there was someone there that early in the morning or that the balloons were red.

Of course, they were red—that was one of the campus colors.

She took a hesitant step towards the hallway, raising her hand in a half-hearted wave. There was no returned greeting, no change of the vacant facial expression she could only faintly see. Nothing but the slight sway of the balloons underneath the flow of cool air coming from the cooling system.

Althea then remembered the email from the previous week announcing the opening of the on-campus career closet for students. She put her hand down, feeling silly. Although she couldn't remember what room the closet was located in, she did remember it was on her floor, hence the now obvious mannequin serving as celebratory décor.

Althea closed the door to her office and started her personal coffee pot. She had nothing against the coffee served in the café. She just liked for her office to smell of dark roast as she got started with her day. Althea thrived in quiet and order. The tasks she left for herself the previous day were piled up in neat stacks along her work table. The books she would be using in class were in their designated sections on her bookshelf, spines pulled to the edge so she could easily grab them on her way to class.

There were many reasons she loved her job at the college, but the main one was that she got her very own office once she became full-time faculty. Years as a contingent professor paid off, and she no longer had to separate her workload for several campuses via different colored tote bags. She could now organize everything inside her little space that served as her home away from home.

Satisfied that everything was in order, she prepared her coffee and thought more about the career closet. She searched for a notepad to write on when an idea struck her. Surely the closet would need donations of plus-sized women's clothing. She had a few nice items she could donate to help a larger number of students get prepared to interview for jobs and enter the workforce with professional clothing.

"It would be best to ask the coordinator how to do that since they're here on campus, anyway," she thought. She picked up her badge and opened her office door. In her doorway stood another mannequin, dressed for success. This one held a sign instead of balloons.

"Help Us Celebrate," shouted to her in bold, red lettering.

When her startled breath caught up to her lungs again, she pulled the form over to the side a few inches, out of her doorway, and onto a solid section of wall. She made sure the sign faced outward rather than inward, the way it was first positioned. Turned that way, no one but her could see the message. She looked both ways down the walkway running in front of her office. No one stood there who she could ask about closet donations.

But where had the mannequin come from so quickly?

Althea turned the corner to an opposite hallway. Halfway down stood another mannequin. Another professional dress. This one held more red balloons and a sign. "The Party is Near…"

She continued walking, encountering well-dressed form after well-dressed form, announcing the grand opening and a celebration —but no actual person she could talk to.

Finally, Althea approached a small corner at the end of the hall. She'd never explored that area of the building, as the door leading there wasn't visible from the main walk. A mannequin outside the door held a sign. "Grand Opening Here."

She felt a quick rush of pride that her administrators had seen the need to help students with career services, free interviews, and work clothing to wear on their job hunts. Rarely did helpful services for students actually manifest into action. She had sat on committee after committee, each promising to evolve into helpful services for students or staff. Most of them dissolved without any resolution.

She hadn't worked on the committee responsible for this, but that was fine. Althea opened the door, ready to find out how she could help and do her part.

The room was dark and colder than the isolated hall outside of it. She squinted, trying to determine the size of the room and where the light switch might be. She hadn't expected the career closet to exist in what seemed to be an actual closet. She ran her hand along the wall near the door, which had completely closed behind her.

"Hello?" she inquired. "I wanted to ask a couple of questions about donations."

Rustling movement sounded right next to her. She could smell dust as the movements increased around her. She turned toward the noise and bumped into something solid that grabbed her with hard, cold arm-like growths.

"Thank you for your willingness to donate. We will happily take all you offer." The hiss resounded inside her head and enveloped her like a whispery hug.

A dim pinprick of light appeared at Althea's eye level. She was surrounded by balloons and signs—and mannequins, shuttling toward her on unbending legs.

"I wanted to ask about donating clothes to the career closet." She tried to make her way back to the door but could no longer feel where it was. More sharp appendages grabbed at her, piercing her skin. Something reached her mouth and ripped out her tongue.

As she gurgled to attempt a scream, she felt a sharp swipe across her throat. Warmth flooded her neck, chest, and stomach moments before a burning slicing started along the front of her torso. She felt moist objects spill from her, sliding down her legs to the floor. Another slash to her head, and her face froze, eyes reduced to slippery orbs hanging down her ripped skin.

"Thank you. Thank you for your donation to your very grand opening."

EIGHT

THE COLLECTOR

*G*irl, if that skirt and them boots don't get that brother to push *forward, you might have to look elsewhere for the attention.*

Maybe.

Tanita put a little extra swing to her hips as she approached the spot where Lucas usually met up with her in the main classroom hall. The movement was easy with the raised heels on the boots, higher than she usually wore when she knew she had to hoof it through the halls and out to and from the parking shuttle. Making that trek would require extra diligence that evening, but it would be worth it if everything turned out the way she wanted it to. She was on a mission to get Lucas to finally ask her out.

Wasn't that the natural next step for them? They already walked together every night. He was a man of few words, and each conversation consisted mostly of Tanita waiting for him to get just the right words to come out of his thick, beautiful lips. She could have simply looked at him the whole time, but he seemed to grow nervous whenever she tried to do that, and fidgeted with his glasses and picked at his 'fro until she said something. Tanita preferred not talk so much, but for the chance to get closer to him, she'd move outside her comfort zone.

It was comforting to have someone to walk out to the parking shuttle after class and chat with on the ride to the parking lot. They'd fallen into step with one another one evening at the beginning of fall term, and now that the holidays were around the corner, Tanita wanted more from the afro-wearing dude who made her heart flutter with the low timbre of his voice and particular choice of sparse conversation. The less he said, the more she wanted to know about him.

You know there's only one way to get as close to him as you're tryna get.
Yes.

She did know his name. She knew what he drove. She memorized his class schedule. That info wasn't particularly sensitive or telling—there were only so many classes anyone on campus in the evenings could be taking, and by the time they came out of class at 10:00 pm every night, theirs were regularly the last two vehicles in the cheap lot.

What was quite telling was how he had started parking his refurbished truck right next to her little car in the far-flung parking lot miles away from the campus. And how he always sat next to her on the shuttle bus each evening, no matter where she decided to sit. These silent moves were important in their relationship progression.

The most important things were that he was strapped for money, just as she was, and wanted a college education like she did, to try and change those financial circumstances. And he was feeling her. She also wanted him to like her the way she liked him, hence the leveling up in her wardrobe. There wasn't a person around who could possibly resist her thick thighs in a mini skirt and high-heeled boots.

"I like your boots." His voice unraveled from his throat like a caress, spoken softly, only for her ears.

"Thank you. I'm glad it's finally cool enough here to wear them."

"Me, too."

Bingo.

Got him.

He stood at the side of the shuttle steps and extended his hand to assist her up the steps, as he usually did. She heard his sharp intake of breath when she dropped her pocketbook on the van floor and bent to pick it up while he stood behind her, waiting to board. Her eyes met those of the shuttle driver, and they shared the universal, "Girl, you got that brother's nose wide open," look.

They remained silent until they'd been seated for a few minutes.

"Do you, uh, wanna come hang out with me tomorrow night, since we don't have class on Fridays?"

"Okay."

He fidgeted with his glasses. "I have to stay at home with my dad that night because his caregiver has the night off. But he'll be medicated, in bed, and we'll have the house to ourselves. We can play some games or find something to watch."

"Cool."

"I'll drop you a pin when I get home tonight." He held his phone out to her, and Tanita's fingers tingled where they touched one another. She hesitated for a moment, then put her phone number in his phone.

"…unless you want me to come pick you up?"

Tanita agreed instantly. "Yes, please. I get a little nervous driving at night when I'm not sure where I'm going."

"No problem. Send me your location when you get in."

"Okay."

Lucas seemed worn out with the effort of finally asking her out and settled on holding her hand. Tanita basked in the warmth of this momentous first, his hand grasping hers for the duration of their ride.

He held her hand again as they walked towards their vehicles. "Make sure you wear this skirt and boots. Or some other high heels."

"Okay. I have other ones."

She wasn't prepared when he suddenly pulled her in for a warm hug. Although she could feel stirrings of desire in her belly, their embrace didn't seem to affect him in the same way. She wasn't worried—he would feel her before tomorrow night was over.

He held her car door open so she could get in. "You're such a teeny, little thing. So sweet."

She struggled to keep her facial expression pleasant as he closed the door. Once she drove off, she gave in to the festering wound inside her soul that his innocent words had dredged up.

"You need to keep your head outta them clouds and put your feet on the ground." Herman Stetson tore at the ink-marked, thin paper he held in his work-roughened hands. The half-bottle of whiskey he had already guzzled down made the task harder than it should have been, and he fumbled with the drawings.

His fumbling allowed plenty of time for Teeny to whimper her grief at losing her beloved pictures to her father's vicious handling. Each tear he made in the paper cut her like a knife, destroying the manifestation of her love for her friends she had poured into the images. The long, painstaking hours she had taken to draw each one, lovingly, melted away in the viciousness of her father's attack.

"Teeny want her friends back!" The little girl's slight body shook each time she repeated the phrase in her small voice, filled with despair.

"Your name ain't Teeny. It's Tanita." Herman threw the chunks of paper onto the floor as he yelled at his daughter. He grabbed her by the shoulders and shook her until her head bobbed back and forth. "You need to grow up! Stop playing these damned make-believe games!"

"It's not pretend! They talk to me. They love me and they not mean to me like you. They don't leave me alone like you do. They know Mama. She sent them. She comes with them sometimes."

Herman stopped his assault momentarily and stared at his eight-year old daughter. "They knew your whore mother? Then I know they ain't no good. Ain't none of y'all bitches no damned good." He shook her harder.

Her head started to hurt, and she became nauseous with the motion her father set for them. From the fog threatening to fully embrace her, she heard the voices come forth.

We do love you. He doesn't. We'll help you.

Her only friends took her outside her body, to float alongside them, so she could no longer feel the physical pain being inflicted on her slight corpus.

The loudest voice was her mother's, and Tanita had never forgotten her loving touch.

After Herman fell asleep in a drunken stupor, his daughter long forgotten, Tanita remembered her friends' promise. She tiptoed into the bathroom and eased her father's straight razor from the medicine cabinet. She winced as she jostled the bruises on her body in her efforts to contort her body and stay quiet.

She stood over her father's sleeping form. He tossed and turned, tortured even in sleep.

You will help him if you slice his neck open with that razor. Set him free. Gain his power for yourself.

Tanita felt a guiding iciness lead her closer to her father, swiping the razor once across his throat, twice. Three times. She moved back away from the blood spray. He fumbled, half awake, already bleeding out. His eyes opened wider when he saw his daughter.

"Sophia?" He gurgled her mother's name, terror replacing surprise. He feebly tried to scramble up the couch, away from his daughter, mouthing his disappeared wife's name until his mouth stopped moving altogether.

Tanita moved closer one last time, avoiding the pools of blood that surrounded her father. The same guiding iciness helped her place the razor in his hand and urged her to return to bed.

The little girl couldn't fully understand the new feeling she held inside her soul. She had always felt loved by her friends and her mother, even when Herman had told her Sophia had left them both —she could still see and feel her, even though she looked different, so how had she left her?—but she had gained and lost upon the death of her father.

He now stood in the corner of her bedroom, just as pained and bitter as he had been in life, his spirit dirty and muddied. Her mother had become more vibrant, even more so than she had been before she disappeared. Tanita felt strong and invincible as her mother became a part of her consciousness.

We will take your father with us. Sophia is now one with you, through his actions, and she will never leave you.

In the years that followed, Tanita began to fully understand what these events had created for her life.

And she wanted more of it.

"I hope you don't mind picking me up here." Tanita waited for Lucas's response, unsure if he was annoyed she didn't give him her address, and opted to have him pick her up from the parking lot on campus instead.

"No problem. I can see you being cautious these days. I could be a serial killer, for all you know." He flashed an uncharacteristic grin, and Tanita tried to relax.

He helped her into his truck, and they settled into what turned out to be a relatively short and quiet ride to Acres Home, a historic community within the Houston city limits. When Lucas pulled his truck into a heavily wooded area, she was surprised to see a nicely kept, older, two-story home appear just beyond the trees.

"Here we are. Home again, home again, jiggety jig."

Tanita giggled, climbing down from the truck into the yard. She followed him into a foyer that looked like it stood still in time, frozen in the 1970s.

"I know it looks like a mausoleum. My pops never upgraded his childhood home in big ways. He always said, 'But it's paid off,' like that made it less ugly." He walked through double doors to the side of what looked like a kitchen and allowed her to enter ahead of him.

"I like the vibe." She took in the modern look of the suite they entered. "This part looks newer." Posters covered every inch of the walls and ceiling, rap artists, metal bands, porn stars, movie posters, book covers. The room looked like a hedonistic ode to decadence in all art forms. Stacks of books on various topics sat on the desk and in the corners of the room. It looked like him. The only thing out of place was the large white rabbit in the cage in the far corner. Seemed a soft type of pet for a guy like Lucas to have. Maybe she didn't know him as well as she thought she instinctively did.

"Yeah, he did change this part up for my mom. She stayed down here to battle cancer. I moved in when she passed."

"I'm sorry to hear you lost her."

"You hungry?" Lucas seemed eager to change the subject, and she allowed it. "We can get something delivered. Or, I have leftover curry in the fridge."

"I'd love some curry! Is it gonna be good?" Tanita teased.

"For sure. If I can't do nothing else, I can burn."

They moved to the kitchen, where Tanita became fascinated with watching his growing confidence as he moved around the room. By the time they ate, she was tied up in knots with anticipation of what the night could bring.

"So what do you like to do when you ain't doing homework?" Lucas posed the question, and Tanita had the idea that her answer would be critically important.

"I like to collect things."

"Word? I'm a bit of a collector, myself, as you can see. What kind of things do you collect?"

She spun her spoon around inside her bowl. "A little of this and that. Mostly things that make me feel good to be around."

Go slow, girl. Don't try to take him too fast.

Right.

"This is so, so good." She licked her lips, and he stared at her. "What?"

He moved to stand in front of where she sat at the counter and took her face in his hands.

"I've dreamed of you here, like this, since we first met." He kissed her softly. "Almost perfect."

"Almost?" Tanita agreed that there was something missing. But she wanted to hear it from him.

"Almost. One thing would make this heaven for us both." He went to the opposite end of the kitchen and drew a large knife from the block. She stood up as he approached her again, her breath caught in her throat. He pressed the handle into her hand and pressed his pelvis against her. The stirrings of his erection startled her.

"What…" she licked her lips, gathering her thoughts, "…do you want me to do with this?" His erection throbbed with her question. Wordlessly, he grabbed her by her empty hand and led her back to his suite of rooms, to the cage in the corner.

"It would be sexy to watch you bend over in those heels and that skirt. And slice into this fucker over and over again." His breathing quickened, and she felt his erection, larger than when they were in the kitchen, threatening to burst from his pants.

"Your pet?" She turned so she was facing him, looking up into his eyes. "You want me to kill your pet? With this?" Tanita motioned to the knife she still held.

Lucas sat down in a chair a couple of feet away from her. "That ain't my pet. I got a pair of them so I could try it myself. Did the first one. It ain't do nothing for me, though. I need somebody else to do it so I can watch. I need you to do it." He began to openly stroke himself, eyes on her.

She stared at the rabbit in the cage and grabbed it by the scruff of its neck. It stared at her with one eye. What was the other eye looking at? She raised the knife. She heard Lucas's breathing change, his hand moving faster along his crotch. Her own body moistened.

Tanita lowered the rabbit. "I'm sorry. I can't."

She watched Lucas as he closed his eyes and let out a ragged breath.

"Maybe if…do you have something I can take for my nerves?"

"Bet. I got you. It's okay if you're nervous. Sexier that you never did this before." He reached into a drawer and pulled out various drugs and paraphernalia. "You want heroin? Weed? Got some vodka somewhere around here if you want a drink."

He got a whole pharmacy over here. You better watch yourself.

For sure.

"That's all pretty heavy duty. I got some Xan in my purse. That okay with you?"

Lucas smiled. "It's all good, baby girl. Whatever you need."

Tanita shook two pills from the bottle she retrieved from her purse. She placed one between her teeth and leaned over onto Lucas's lap to press her lips to his. He took the pill from her and dry swallowed. She then placed the second in her mouth and followed his actions. He pulled her into his lap so he could kiss her more fully.

She straddled him and did a slow grind with her panties pressed against his jeans. His full erection did not return, but he maintained a slight showing. It was gonna get hotter as soon as the pills kicked in.

They necked and petted until Tanita was ready for more.

"Don't you wanna get into some real action?" She asked while she was still straddling him. She needed to gauge his reaction.

"What you mean?"

"The rabbit is little. Don't you wanna know what it would be like with something...bigger?"

His erection throbbed, back to full force.

"Bigger like what?"

Tanita had his full attention. She pulled a condom from her bra and told him to slide it on.

"Didn't you say your father is sick upstairs?"

"Yeah." Lucas's gaze bore into her face. "So?"

"So, you ever think about how you could help him? He must be in a lot of pain." Her words needed to sink in. She nipped at his earlobe. "It would take a while to get him done. We could take our sweet time." Tanita began her slow grind into his latex-clad pelvis again, allowing the images her words conjured to do their magic inside his head.

Lucas groaned. "We'd be helping him."

"Yes."

He's almost there, girl. Hold steady.

Okay.

"Have you ever been this hard before?"

"Nnn…no. Let's do it."

Tanita rose from her perch and allowed him to lead her up the stairs. He stumbled along, and she was worried he was changing his mind.

"That Xan got me going down. Hard to walk with a hard-on like this. I'm all the way up. We gotta hurry."

They quietly entered a room at the top of the stairs. In the dim nightlight, Tanita saw the prone, slight shape of a body lying in the bed before them. She tiptoed closer to the bed, and Lucas followed, pressing against her buttocks, rigid. Ready.

She raised the knife and plunged it into the man's neck, leaving him no time to scream. Only a garbled gurgle escaped his throat. Lucas pulled her panties to the side and entered her body, plunging in and out of her wetness at the same pace she sliced at his father. Blood spurted around them, and Lucas spurted inside her as her body tightened around his, her own release sudden and violent.

Lucas did not become soft after their frenzied mating. Instead, he continued to drive inside her body, leaning her forward until his father's life force spread around and over the both of them.

Finally, they collapsed at the foot of the bed, breathing ragged. Tanita struggled to slide from underneath Lucas. She got him to stand and stagger a couple of feet away from the bed before he stumbled to the floor. She climbed on top of his body, impaling herself on his erection again.

"Good?" She bent to kiss him.

"Never had nothing like that before."

"I know. Let's level up." Tanita plunged the knife into his chest, relishing the shock that crossed his face.

"Wha—?"

"I was just getting started. Your father was a bonus I hadn't expected. He feels good in my collection. Decent man, he was. He ain't even watching the rest of this."

"Dad?" Lucas focused his weak gaze just past Tanita's shoulder. "Who are these people? What the fuck?" His speech faltered, mostly due to the muscle relaxer she'd given him. And the pain. The pain was what she wanted most.

Ride him, girl.

"You see them? Good. You're gonna join them directly." She swerved side to side on his member, feeling her next orgasm just beyond her reach.

"Joe and Lo are twins. Our threesome was supposed to be us licking a little blood from each other, but I took all theirs." She moaned.

Work that shit.

"See the woman there? That's Sandy. She was an amazing lay. Screamed the whole time I stabbed her in the stomach and rode her face." In and out. She sliced the knife across his throat.

"That dude is Terrance. Loved pain. Came inside me right before his dying breath. He likes to give me advice on future collections. He told me you'd be good, but I didn't know you'd be this delicious." Up and down.

Bring us your pleasure. Yes!

She stabbed the knife into the wound she made in Lucas's neck, keeping the tempo with her pelvis. She rode the waves of her peak, moving in time with the slowed beating of his heart, squeezing her last desire from the finality of his life.

Tanita rose from his body, sliding the condom off him.

She directly addressed his spirit that materialized in the room next to the others. "You thought you were introducing me to the pleasures of blood and murder. Turned out I was the one hipping you to some new shit on that tip."

She removed her shoes and went back downstairs to clean herself up and remove herself from the house. She bundled up her eating dishes, along with her clothes, and the knife she'd used.

"I'm gonna take your truck back to the parking lot to pick up my car, Lucas. Then I'll head to the gas station. Chick was eyeballing me last time I was there. Maybe I can get her to join our collection later."

Tanita left Acres Homes fuller than when she first came to the neighborhood, stronger. Sated for a moment.

Let's go rest.

Yes. Rest.

NINE

SWEET SUNDAY SUPPER SMILE

S KRITCH.

Me and Sissy startled.

"Wood rats beneath the floor. Eat," Mama said. We ate our daily rice with watery gravy.

Mama stayed hungry.

SKRITCH. SKRITCH.

They stayed hungry.

Me and Sissy woke each other up every night when one of us had to go to the restroom. We would never go alone because we knew *they* were there in our small four-plex unit. In the walls. Under the floors. In the ceiling. So far, we hadn't seen them, and we had no idea what they might look like.

We also never knew when they might decide to stop hiding.

Mama took us to church on Sundays, and we always glanced at the large rectangular holes at the bottom of our building. We asked why the holes were there.

"Probably to help with flooding."

We didn't understand the idea of flooding just yet. We did understand that the holes looked like eyes. And we understood that through those eyes, we saw *their* eyes some mornings, watching, waiting.

When we got to church, Mama put on her Sweet Sunday Supper smile. Sissy and me called it that because when she smiled that smile, the old people in the church gave us candy and smiled back at us. Then they sent us home with a bag of food that Mama would fix for supper.

SKRITCH. SKRITCH. SKRITCH.

The scratching grew louder, and Mama started to worry about the food the church gave us being eaten by the rats. We tried to tell her again that they weren't rats, but she wouldn't listen to us. She called the landlord over.

"I don't see any evidence of rats anywhere here." He shut off his big flashlight and grinned at Mama. She didn't smile back at him, and we were glad she didn't give him that special smile.

"Can you at least put down some poison outside? I can't have them getting in here to my babies. And our food."

He looked at us then, a scary gleam in his eyes. "Yes, those are some pretty babies you got there. Just like their mama."

"Don't you look at my babies. And you better get something done because otherwise, I'll call the city on you."

He shook his head and moved toward the front door. "You don't have to be like that. I'll put something out."

She told us we didn't have to worry about the rats while we waited for the landlord to make good on his word. She patted the lumpy stick she kept near our bed in case Daddy broke into the apartment again, drunk and loud.

"I'll keep you safe with this."

SKRITCH. SKRITCH.

We ain't have to worry about Daddy no more, but she didn't know that. The only reason we knew was because one day on the way to church, Sissy had seen something shiny in the dirt underneath one of the building eyes. On our way back, I had distracted Mama so Sissy could go get it. It was Daddy's necklace, the one he said he got in the Army. I read his name from it to Sissy, and we looked at each other, silently acknowledging what we both knew to be true.

They got him.

They ain't no rats.

They ain't staying down there forever.

The day the landlord came to place the poison, he knocked on our door. Mama had to go to work, and we were out of school. She told us to never open the door for anyone when she was gone. So we stayed quiet and watched as the landlord let himself in with his key. He was as surprised to see us as we were him. We kept our attention on the television.

"Where's your mama?"

We stared at him, Sissy nestling deeper into my side on the couch.

He came inside the apartment and closed the door, looking all around outside before he did.

"Your mama out? Y'all are here alone?"

We still didn't answer him.

He came and sat down on the couch at the other end. "I wanna be your friend. Can't we be nice to each other?" He licked his lips. "I did what your mama asked and put out some poison, even though ain't no rats here." He scooted closer to the middle of the couch.

SKRITCH. SKRITCH. SKRITCH.

His smile fell when he finally heard the loud scratching. He wrinkled his eyebrows. "What the..."

Sissy and me kept our eyes on the corner of the small living room where the sheetrock began to come down in small clouds of dust.

The first one came out, quickly followed by another and another. A group of furry things swarmed from the hole and crawled over and pulled the landlord off the couch before he could get a scream out.

They tore at his flesh with long claws coming from their multiple legs and bit with teeth longer and sharper than we'd ever seen. Blood matted their grayish-brown fur, and we could barely see their large, red eyes in the mess they made. They even ate the bones, cracking them with strong jaws.

As the others finished up, one of them lumbered over to Sissy and me. It stood up on two of its legs and watched us, close enough that we could smell it. Sissy started to cry, and I hugged her closer. The creature tilted its head to the side and then started to move its mouth. The corners slowly lifted in what I recognized as an attempted smile. Not nearly as pretty as Mama's Sweet Sunday Supper Smile, but an honest try.

"Look, Sissy, it won't hurt us. It's trying to be nice."

Sissy sniffled and looked at the creature. It smiled again and reached out with a clawed leg to pat each of us gently on the head.

It returned to the others, where they had completely cleaned up any trace of their meal. On their way back through the hole, they also cleaned up the sheetrock debris, leaving a neat hole in their wake.

Sissy and me looked at each other and didn't need to speak. We gave each other our Sweet Sunday Supper smiles and turned the channel to another cartoon.

TEN
SUFFER THE LITTLE CHILDREN

*N**ow, she knows it's way too cold for those babies to be in that water like that!*

Rae sucked her teeth and shook her head as she pulled her sweater tighter around her. She stopped her beach stroll to stare at the woman on the sand in the distance, watching the four little kids tumble in the chilly waters of Surfside Beach.

They're gonna catch their death.

She didn't see a vehicle anywhere near them, so she thought they might be renting one of the houses along the shore.

Tourists.

Her babies were long grown up, and she thought about how she'd always felt like folks were judging how she was parenting them when they were young. She didn't want to be *that nosy old woman*, but from where she stood, the woman seemed awfully young.

Besides, Rae wasn't that old…only middle-aged. And the kids outnumbered the other woman, four to one. Rae's husband, Tim, had worked as a long-distance truck driver throughout their marriage, so she was mostly left alone with their kids.

Not that her kids could be bothered to remember how she'd pretty much raised them without their beloved dad's physical presence or help. He had only financed their household expenses and performed drive-by visits, where he spent his off days running other errands rather than helping with the kids and things that needed to be done inside the house. She did all the hard work of parenting and managing the household, but the kids still hardly called or visited her since Tim had passed on two years prior.

"Maybe she's on her own, too." Rae decided she'd just take a slight detour close to where they were playing and see if she could offer a hand in getting the kids wrangled and out of the water. She didn't have any towels with her, and they didn't seem to, either, but they could figure something out.

The first thing she noticed as she walked within speaking distance of the little family was how the kids completely ignored her. The woman turned slightly to face her, and Rae secondarily noted her slow movements encased within the full sweatsuit she wore, complete with the pulled-up hood. She didn't want to be angry with the woman without knowing the whole story, but it seemed pretty selfish that she was covered up and the babies weren't.

The little ones wore tiny summer swimsuits, perfect for the scorching sun that would bear down relentlessly in their region in another few weeks, but which had yet to make much of an appearance in the unusually cool spring they currently enjoyed.

"Hello!" Rae worked to keep her voice cheerful. The children continued to splash in the light brown surf.

"Hi."

The single gravelly word seemed forced across the younger woman's vocal cords. She had already turned back to watch the children. Not before Rae had seen the dark bruises underneath both eyes and the slow but furtive motion to pull the strings of the hoodie tighter around her injured neck.

Her slow movements, bruises, and hesitance told a desperate story that almost brought Rae to tears. *Poor girl! Her man beat her real bad.*

She cleared her own throat and spoke again, keeping the pity at bay so the girl wouldn't bolt away.

"They sure are full of energy! I wish I had some of that right about now."

No response from the mother.

"My babies were never that energetic when they were little. Aren't they cold? How old are they?" She took a step closer to the woman. Close enough to see her shudder. Not close enough to get her talking.

She wrapped her arms tight around her torso. "I can help you gather them up and get them out of the water, if you want. I'm sure they can be a handful." Rae forced a smile onto her face, despite the knot that grew in her stomach when she thought the woman still wouldn't respond.

"You have no idea. They never let me rest. Never."

The words spat from between the full lips startled Rae. It wasn't just the vehemence the utterance held. The underlying tone almost escaped her, but not quite.

The woman was afraid of her children.

"Oh, toddlers can be real hellions, but they can be brought to heel."

The other woman had already turned her gaze towards the children again.

"Not them. They do what they want. They know I can't stop them."

She shuddered again, and Rae followed suit. The air on the shore grew chillier as they stood in silence for a few moments before Rae tried again.

"Do you have towels for them? We can bundle them up and get y'all inside."

The woman furrowed her brows and looked around on the ground where she stood. She closed her eyes briefly, sagging deep into the sweatsuit so that Rae barely heard the rest of her words.

"They're fine. They'll come out when they get ready. Thank you."

Rae wanted to say more, but was interrupted by the oldest girl, who appeared to be around seven years old.

"Who are you?" Pale, bluish gray eyes, much lighter than the color of the sky they stood underneath, bore into hers. Three more pairs of the same eyes turned to her, as well, and all movement in the water stopped. Her siblings were obviously younger than she, although Rae couldn't tell exactly how old any of them really were.

Rae held the girl's gaze and felt as if she was falling into the depths of emotionless pools. She had only seen eyes anywhere near that color once before. When she was a girl, she and her cousin came upon the corpse of their neighbor's dog that had died in the woods behind their grandmother's house. Its eyes had been a brilliant brown in life. In death, the gray of the unknown beyond had tainted their brilliance.

The children's mother moved more quickly than she had the whole time Rae had been watching them.

"This is a nice lady who offered to help us. She's going to continue on her way because we're okay." She turned to face Rae, dark eyes imploring her to agree.

Against her better judgment, Rae did so.

"Yes. I thought you might be cold, and I wanted to help your Mommy get you out of the water. But I'll leave you to your fun."

The baby toddled toward Rae in that speedy way only toddlers could move. Before Rae could back away, the baby wrapped her arms around her legs, sending jolts of icy pain through Rae's skin.

"Jasmine! Did you find Mommy a shell like we saw on television? Come help me, baby girl."

The little arms released Rae, but the children's gazes did not falter.

Rae stumbled and then ran back the same way she had come, unsure of what had happened but convinced that even if the family needed her help, they certainly didn't want it.

Something wasn't right about those kids.

Rae had tried her best to forget about the sad woman and the odd little kids until she ran right into the two oldest ones in the convenience store later that evening.

"Where're your parents?" The store clerk asked the boy and girl as he looked around for an adult to claim them.

"Mommy's right outside in the car. On the side part." The boy spoke more clearly than his appearance as a small six-year-old would have belied. He continued to stare at the man as he held out the bill in his tiny hand to pay for the large, brilliantly colored bag of potato chips on the counter. His sister stood slightly behind him, in silence.

There were no cars parked on the side of the store. And Rae didn't see their mother anywhere.

They're trying to protect their mother.

Perhaps she had sent them to the store alone. Or maybe she was unable to stop them from leaving if something had happened to her.

Her heart broke for the little family. She hadn't seen a father with them earlier, but those bruises on their mother hadn't appeared from nowhere.

The cashier started to shake his head slowly from side to side as he reached for the phone on the side counter.

"They're with me." Rae walked up to stand directly behind the children. She wasn't really being a busybody if the kids were in danger of having the police called on them and Child Protective Services inserted in their and their mother's lives. The younger woman was likely doing the best she could, and Rae couldn't stand to see her punished for a minor misjudgment.

Still, something could have happened to the small children as they traveled to and from the store alone. Rae decided she would walk them back home. "And I may as well check on their mother while I'm there, too," she muttered to herself.

The children paid for their snack, and Rae paid for her bottle of water. They waited patiently beside the door for her to complete her transaction, their chilly, pale eyes trained on the cashier, who still shook his head, also muttering under his breath. Rae watched as large beads of sweat appeared suddenly on his forehead and rolled down the sides of his face. She grabbed her change from him before those beads could drop on the bills.

"Let's go." She hadn't expected them to easily do as she said, but they surprised her, and the two kids padded obediently beside her, one on each side, their little feet making quiet slaps on the pavement. They also allowed her to grab their hands as they crossed the street back to the beach side. Rae was shocked by the initial iciness of their little fingers and reminded herself that they were small children outside in cool weather and it would take a while for them to warm up.

"Does Mommy know you two went to the store?"

"Yes." The girl spoke up.

"Was she too tired to go with you?"

"She was laying down."

Rae nodded. "Do you mind if I walk you home and check on her?"

"Okay."

"You'll have to show me where you live."

As the children guided her toward their house, Rae was struck with sadness at how much the babies loved their mother and wanted to protect her. Her own adult children had forgotten she even existed, and she had to text them constantly to get minimal updates on them and her grandchildren.

She missed the time when they were young and when they needed and loved her. She was always with them, and she had sacrificed so much for them. She and Tim had grown apart during their childhood, and yet, she stayed with him so the children could have stability. Tim hadn't noticed the distance between them and probably believed up until the day he died that they were just like any other married couple.

The children slowed down in front of a large, expensive-looking beach house close to where she had first seen them. The two-story home loomed ominously in the twilight of the waning sun. No porch light welcomed them. The little boy went up the stairs in front of Rae, and his sister went behind her.

As they entered the front door, the smell hit Rae in the face. It wasn't overpowering, but it was largely unpleasant. She struggled to see in the dim room, wanting to open the windows to let in fresh, salted air from the ocean but also needing light to assess her surroundings. Movement from across the room caught her eye and then disappeared in the darkness as the girl closed the door behind her.

"I know you're hungry. I'll get up and feed you all in a little while."

Rae recognized the woman's voice, even tinged with the exhaustion she heard from her. "Hi, it's me again. Rae. From the beach earlier. I walked the kids…"

"No! What are you doing here? Leave now." Urgency slightly raised the young mother's voice, and Rae walked sideways, feeling along the wall until she found the light switch and flipped it.

Her brain wasn't ready to accept what the light revealed. The warm-up suit was the same, but the woman in it looked much older than she had earlier. Dry, wrinkled skin covered her face, giving her the visage of a skull covered in leather. A skeletal hand waved feebly in Rae's direction.

"Please."

Rae didn't know what the woman was imploring her to do. Then she realized it wasn't her the request was directed at.

The two youngest children appeared from around a corner and stood with their two older siblings.

"Mommy's tired. Please let me rest. Someone else can take care of you."

One of the toddlers spoke up. "I give Mommy Daddy juice." She stretched out her hands toward her mother, and the woman recoiled.

"I just want to die. I'm already dead. Please, let me rest." The woman slumped down into the couch once again.

"Mommy, you're the only grown-up we have left. The Daddy juice is almost gone, and we don't know where to find more." The oldest girl turned her gaze to Rae. "Daddy hurt Mommy really bad when he put his hands around her neck. Then we made him sleep so we could wake Mommy up."

"But she wouldn't stay awake unless we kept giving her Daddy juice," the oldest boy continued.

"They won't let me rest. I slept for just a moment, and they brought me right back. And they keep doing it over and over again. I don't want to be here anymore, but they keep bringing me back." The last of the woman's words came out in a croak.

"We could let Mommy rest if you will take care of us." Four pairs of eyes settled on Rae.

She found her voice. "I can't take care of you. I … I don't understand what's going on here. Let me get some help."

"No one else can help. We already gave you some Daddy juice, and it's working. You have to stay with us and take care of us now."

Rae's mind raced back to the wet embrace from the toddler on the beach and the gripping of her hands by the two older children. She remembered the iciness that coursed through her at their touch.

She knew they told the truth. They had given her *something*. She didn't fully understand what the something was, but it didn't matter right then.

"Where do you get the Daddy juice?"

"From Daddy. In the bedroom closet."

"Can we let Mommy rest for a little bit while you take me to see Daddy?"

She allowed the toddlers to grasp her hands that time. The chill from their hands stabbed through her until it no longer sent shockwaves up her arms.

They opened the closet in a back bedroom to reveal the dried-out corpse of their father, withered almost completely to dust.

There would be so much to figure out in being their caregiver. They seemed too young to understand where their gift came from, so she had no idea how to help them manage it. But they needed her. They were babies. She no longer had any babies, so she needed them, too.

"Did you just give me the last Daddy juice?'

"Yes. You're nice." The baby girl stuck her thumb in her mouth and leaned against Rae's legs.

"When I go to sleep like Mommy, will you have to find more juice from somewhere to give me?"

"I think so." The oldest girl furrowed her eyebrows. "But maybe you won't sleep like that for a long, long time since we gave you Daddy juice before you went to sleep."

Rae guessed the girl might be right. "Why don't we go tell Mommy she can sleep now? That will make her so happy."

"Okay." The kids ran down the hallway back into the living room, Rae following behind them, wondering if there was any food in the house she could make them for dinner.

ELEVEN
ENDLESS POSSIBILITIES

I *would hate for all this to be the last thing I see if I die in my sleep tonight.*

Drea squeezed past the group taking pictures in the ship's narrow hallway, trying not to wrinkle her nose in distaste. She couldn't begrudge the tourists their desire to capture their trip in photos so they could remember their experiences. What she hated with more passion than she thought she could muster at her advanced age was the gaudy, glaring décor the ocean liner designers decided to foist on them all. She stumbled as the ship lurched from side to side, roughly, and she lost her footing.

Even the ship was attacking her now.

Loud colors that clashed with her sensibilities screamed from every inch of the ship. Glittery walls and accoutrements shone brightly, painfully so, giving her a headache and a pain in her butt, all at once. She couldn't understand why the choices presented were made. Nothing was cohesive, and yet, nothing was purposefully abstract, either.

How could surroundings so boisterous promote relaxation? How could bulbous blobs of clownishly colored glass melded onto flat, icy flat glass backings promote warmth and safety? Except...she had reached out to touch one of the blobs when they first got on the ship the previous day, and it had felt warm. Hot, even. Startled, she snatched her hand back when she thought she felt it move beneath her hand.

"Cedric? Do you see these?"

"What are you talking about?" Her husband was already walking far ahead of her, straight to the bar in the middle of the entryway. She looked around at her fellow passengers. No one else was examining the decorations. They weren't touching the glass.

The glass wasn't touching them.

She dismissed the sensation, chalking it up to her state of mind at having been herded on the trip in the first place by the man she no longer wanted to stay married to, despite the fact that they had a currently ongoing twenty-five-year marriage.

Not for much longer.

Drea ground her teeth and groaned as the incessant and unsettling hum she'd been hearing since boarding continued to plague her. It reminded her of the hum of electricity, but louder and grating. She had always loved thunderstorms and felt invigorated by the electrical impulses travelling through the air. This hum didn't give her that same comfort.

It hurt.

She rubbed her temples and decided to find a staff member to ask about it as soon as she found someone. The phone in their cabin didn't work, and she needed to report that, as well. The vessel made another sudden pitch, and her last meal threatened to move upward from her stomach. The water had been rough since embarkation, and it was getting worse the further out into the ocean they traveled. Drea had never been on a ship before, but she determined that she'd never get her sea legs. Not that she wanted them if it meant more of this extraneous movement she didn't like.

A resonant voice came over the loudspeaker as she tentatively made her way further along the hallway, holding on to the doorways along the wall for stability.

"This is your ship's captain speaking. The water is unexpectedly rough, and we advise all passengers to safely and, in an orderly manner, retire early to your cabins for your well-being. We will expand the room service offerings, but request that you only place necessary orders for the safety of our crew. We apologize for any inconvenience this may cause and are working with the cruise line to process vouchers for missed excursions tomorrow and provide an inconvenience restitution. We will keep you posted on traveling conditions throughout the evening."

That Cedric would choose such a tacky and boisterous setting as a touristy cruise ship for what he was dramatically calling their Reawakening as a Couple was just like him. He held these grand ideas about everything and lived for the drama and the appearances. Their marriage had always been no different—all show, no substance. She had bought into his charming showmanship when they were dating and during the early years of their marriage, back when she had been so in love. She would have followed him anywhere.

She had literally followed him anywhere...everywhere. When he'd declared he wanted to be an actor and that he had the magic formula to guarantee success, she'd packed up their beloved Texas cottage and unpacked in the tiny apartment in Los Angeles that followed. He worked at becoming the next best thing in Hollywood for a whole two years. Then, a more earnest—according to Cedric—endeavor called to his soul from Wall Street in New York City. They picked up and moved again, that time to a drafty old apartment half the size of the apartment in LA. It always smelled of tobacco and smoke from the cigar shop they lived two stories above.

Drea stayed in and out of the hospital with her asthma, having gotten exponentially worse with the drafts and the smoke exacerbating it. Her medical bills ate up most of the financial gains they could have made. But it didn't help that Cedric never brought in the kind of money he claimed was theirs for the taking. By then, she'd begun to question his plans for their family.

"When will we be settled, Cedric?"

"This ain't about you changing your mind about having a baby, is it?" He liked to answer her questions with questions of his own. It was an admirable trait for a finance guy or a salesperson or an entertainer. It was a terrible attribute for a husband.

"No, I still don't want kids. But do we have to have kids to be stable? To stay in one place long enough to put down real roots?" She had been hopeful then. Still loved her husband, with the prospect of spending the rest of her life with him.

"Maybe we should have a kid. You can't get a job. I don't want you to work, anyway. Maybe you need something to do while I'm out hustling. I'm gonna hit it big. I know it."

"I have plenty to do with constantly packing and unpacking. What I need is a chance to make a real home for us."

For me.

"It'll come. Just stick with me." He brought her chin up so her eyes met his and placed a confident kiss on her lips.

That was the first time his kiss failed to warm her the way it had before. It wasn't the last.

Drea sighed. She'd stuck with him, always, up to then. They stayed in New York for three years, her health growing much worse before Cedric announced they were moving to Chicago. That lasted six years before he uprooted them yet again. They landed back in the South, in New Orleans. Drea fell in love with the row house he'd purchased for them. For the first time ever, she planted a garden and the citrus trees she'd always longed for. She hummed as she painted the walls and learned how to perform minor renovations. Driving up to their home after she returned from errands brought her immense pride.

Finally home.

Cedric seemed to lean into his role as the safety manager for one of the local chemical plants. He talked incessantly about his earning potential and what they'd do with all the money. She was happy for him. For them. As they passed year seven there, she'd begun to feel like she just might be able to love her husband again. Drea couldn't put her finger on when, exactly, she had fallen out of love and begun to stew in the resentment of being unheard and unattended for years. Maybe they would be okay after all.

Then came the day Cedric flew into their wonderful little home with that unholy glisten in his eyes that she recognized as wanderlust. She tensed up on the couch where she sat, slamming her teacup down on the coffee table a bit harder than she'd planned.

Cedric didn't flinch at the loud noise. He was in his own little world, as always. "Babe, I have the best news!" He prattled on and on about Oregon, something. West coast, another thing. Before he stopped his animated soliloquy, Drea interrupted.

"I'm not moving again."

His lips continued to move until she yelled.

"I'm not moving!"

Cedric finally broke from his self-focused litany and looked at her as if she had sprouted an additional head. "What's wrong with you?"

His confusion might have been endearing if it hadn't been his default for the past few years. Cluelessness in a middle-aged man with responsibilities was ultimately a bad thing.

She stood up. "I'm sick and tired of you not listening to me. You never ask me what I want, what I need. You've done this our whole marriage, and I'm over it."

They stood in the living room, staring at each other. Cedric finally lowered his gaze. She refused to back down. His shoulders slumped, and he walked slowly to their bedroom. That night, she slept in the guest bedroom.

When she awakened the next morning, Cedric was gone. He left a note indicating he was moving to Oregon, and they could have a long-distance marriage. He promised to continue paying the bills at their home and would visit every few months.

Drea accepted the arrangement for what it was. He wasn't abandoning her, but she was already one foot out the door on their marriage.

She used the time he spent away from home to enroll in law school. There weren't many jobs she could perform that her debilitating asthma would allow her to physically work for long periods, but as a lawyer, she could basically set her own hours and still earn a living wage. She had also developed a burning desire to help women in divorce proceedings to get fair outcomes. The training would prove useful for when she initiated her own divorce.

Drea understood Cedric's financial assistance could run out as soon as he got a wild hair to do something else with himself. She was under no delusions that he would ever come back to their home. And she was fine with that. But she couldn't yet support herself, so she worked extra hard to get done with her degree on time, as quickly as possible.

The right time to tell Cedric about the divorce hadn't come in the three years since he had moved away. She'd just graduated from the program and already had a job with a local firm lined up. She wanted to tell him, wanted to finally start her own life, her own way.

I will tell him soon.

Before she knew it, he'd breezed into town, pushed her to pack a suitcase and medications for a week, and gotten her into the car.

"We're going on a trip."

"This will be a new beginning for us."

"It'll only be a week."

"It'll be fun."

Drea went along with him. She hadn't been on a trip in years, and she did want to celebrate her recent accomplishments, even if she wasn't yet ready to share them with Cedric. Until they pulled up at the port and parked, she'd entertained fleeting thoughts—wishes?—that he'd chosen somewhere fun, something she would enjoy, for them to do.

Then, reality hit. He had never taken her wants or needs into consideration before. The trip was more of the same old same.

Now she was stuck in the middle of the ocean with crowds of

strangers, surrounded by dangerously rough waters and a quarantine circumstance. She had already gingerly made it to the main foyer on their floor and felt her way along the glass walls enclosing the elevators. Drea would follow the captain's orders and return to her room, but she wanted to get a staff member to tell them about their phone first. She had asked Cedric to tell someone when he headed out earlier that evening, but he wouldn't remember. She'd have to take care of it herself, like always.

Her stabilizing hand on the wall began to move. Drea used her other hand to place it against the same wall to prevent her impending fall. Except she wasn't falling. She held her breath for the few seconds her impaired lungs would allow and tried to focus on what was happening. How long had she been out of her room? Four minutes? Five? It had seemed like forever, and the pain inside her head grew until it throbbed in time with the pulsating glass blobs that covered every glass surface on the ship.

The ones underneath her hands grew warmer and melted until they ran down the glass, covering her palms. She wanted to scream, but she couldn't. People swarmed around her, running back to their rooms. No one else touched the walls.

No one touched or looked at the ceilings, either, where more colored glass protrusions slid from their flat anchorings, dripping in her direction.

Drea staggered back towards her cabin, stabilized by the throngs of passengers congesting the small hallways. She shook her hands, and the molten glass remained. Its counterparts continued their singular journey towards her.

"Help me. Please. Do you see this?" None of her fellow shipmates answered her. No one looked at her.

By the time she made it back to her room, she had to hold onto the bolted-down furniture to keep from falling. The glass never left her palms, even when she slammed them against the wooden surfaces.

The hum grew louder until it was a low, timbered roar, reverberating deep in her belly. She watched the agitated waves cresting higher and higher alongside the ship, for as far away as she could see them.

Something is terribly and irrevocably wrong.

Drea made her way to the balcony door and used her knees to help her open the door that threatened to slam shut on her in the strong winds. The glass on her palms ran down her forearms, covering her skin in its warmth.

I don't want to die. I haven't lived yet.

She pressed herself against the balcony door, gripping the supporting posts to stand as straight as she could. Drea had lived her whole life being scared. Scared to trigger her asthma. Scared to decline Cedric's marriage proposal. Scared to leave when she no longer loved him.

I won't be afraid anymore.

She couldn't feel the tears on her face in the onslaught of salt-water splashing from the ocean, drenching everything. The colored glass soon covered her shoulders. She looked down at the floor of the balcony as other colors flowed onto her feet, up her legs. The warmth cocooned her, eased her breathing. Drea should have been wheezing with the panic that threatened to well up inside her, but she'd never breathed more clearly in her life.

Underneath the waves, a large, luminous orb reflected the light of the full moon. She watched as something gargantuan, something ancient, broke the hostile surface of the ocean and emerged. Scale by scale, tentacle by tentacle, her mind had no reference for what she witnessed.

"You can remain." None of these discordant voices were her own. They were a sonorous chorus of numerous voices coming from the glass covering her body.

"Accept the one true god."

"You are chosen."

Drea met the emergent eye with her own gaze, the only thing left uncovered by the glass. The ship bucked, leaning almost horizontally in the water. The god held her stare. The roar faded out as her ears filled.

"Accept us."

"Live again."

"Live forever."

The body continued to rise from the ocean, turning the ship over yet again.

"I accept." Drea had previously accepted far less for herself. She embraced the offering of something that couldn't possibly be as restrictive as her life had been to that point.

Forever home.

Drea's last cognizant thought before the glass covered her eyes was relief at the exaltation her spirit engaged in with the substance and deity she acquiesced to. She rose, past the height of the divine being, past the full moon, past the stars—into the beyond of endless possibilities.

TWELVE
SKINNY MINNIE

"I wish I could be as skinny as you, eating like you do," isn't the compliment folks believe it to be. It's pretty insulting for various reasons, the main one being they never ask or notice how I feel about my weight and body before commenting like that. And it's damned rude. Don't they think I wanna be bootylicious with dangerous curves that stop traffic the way the sisters I see walking down the street do, boobs and ass for days? Why wouldn't I wanna have to tell people I'm in conversation with that my eyes are higher than where their gaze would linger down below?

"So eat a sandwich or something," the smart asses say when I call them on their insensitivity. I eat a lot of sandwiches and a whole lot of everything. I eat everything that doesn't eat me first, like my grandma used to say. Man, I eat more than a pack of teenagers raiding the family fridge right after coming through the door from school. If it's high in calories, I eat it. Pizza, fried foods, bread by the loaf. Pasta with all the sauce. Rich desserts. Ice cream by the half-gallon. Red meat. Greasy dishes. But nothing sticks.

That's because they take it.

They've figured out how to siphon the food right out of my stomach without them being inside the acid-filled organ. They only leave me enough to minimally sustain my body.

I don't know how many there are, but it seems like quite a few. I can feel them moving around all the time, full of energy from my high-calorie, maximum fat diet. They don't seem to ever sleep. Sometimes I get nauseous from their constant movement inside my torso, but I mostly don't throw up.

I've only thrown up a couple of times in my whole life. It's a helluva mindfuck because I can feel them constantly—they never rest or pause–but their movements don't show up on the outside of my belly. They hide in ways babies in utero can't, perfectly evil machinations and devilment of the demented parasites they are.

They've shown themselves to me on two occasions. The first time was when I tried to drink bleach to poison them. One of them broke into my stomach, blinding pain stabbing through my body, causing me to double over and fall onto the floor. It climbed up my esophagus, up through my throat, its anger apparent in the way it unnecessarily stretched the inflexible tubing on its way up and out. I tried to continue swallowing around it, to gulp it down, too, but it used something that felt like soft rubber to block the liquid from going down the tube it invaded so harshly.

It clawed at my throat and pushed the bleach out, back into my mouth, out from between my lips. I didn't see the spiny bristles protruding from its skin that were piercing my tongue and cheeks until I threw up, and the creature fell out in the pool of refuse, reeking of bleach and old spaghetti sauce.

I scrambled up from my prone position and scooted backward toward the laundry room wall, watching it the whole time. Webbed appendages flapped around in the vomit like a popped balloon caught in a dog's mouth, wet and shiny. Limp. The light reflected off the spikes still emerging from a slender, pink, snake-like body.

It tried to move toward me but slowed with each passing second until it came to a stop. It flopped onto its back and waved the webs frantically, a grotesque mimicry of a dying cockroach struggling to breathe through poison. It focused three empty, black holes towards me.

"Do not do that again," it hissed through one hole, working to produce the sound. I squealed; I'd never heard them speak before, not even to each other.

"We will always stop you." The last hiss died away, the body deflating and melting where it lay, spikes emulsifying into a small pile of pink goo.

The others wreaked havoc inside my body when it expired, apparently grieving their dead sibling. I still couldn't see their movements from outside, but I felt their frantic prodding and bucking. I wanted to vomit again, but I knew it would be useless for me to try. I could only put something into my stomach or force it out if they allowed me to.

The last time they showed themselves was after I sliced my stomach open at home. I wanted them out, and they evaded detection by every means doctors were willing to try before writing me off as crazy. I begged them to do something about the creatures, and they just shook their heads and gave me mental health referrals.

I purchased a straight razor through the mail so they wouldn't be able to watch me purchase it in a store. I had no idea how they saw stuff, but they seemed to know when I did certain things.

Before they could discover my intentions, I sliced a deep gash across my belly. My determination to get the creatures out dulled the pain to where I didn't feel much, until various webs came reaching out through the blood, grabbing the edges of my slick skin and pulling them roughly back into place. I felt a searing sensation, and my stomach was being pinched hard. Soon, the incision remained, but the bleeding stopped.

One unfortunate creature hadn't been able to scramble back inside and lay on the floor, dying a more serene death than the last one I had seen, but dying, nonetheless.

"We will never let you kill yourself...or us."

I slid to the floor, pain radiating from my perfectly sealed skin. I believed them. It would be a waste of time to go to more doctors. Even if I told them the wound was self-inflicted, they'd only keep me temporarily on a psychological hold and send me back home. The creatures would hide and relish in the feedings the hospital would make sure I got until then.

I was stuck with them until they were done with me, destined to remain starved, nauseated, and skinny for the duration.

THIRTEEN
HER HEART'S DESIRE

I f Layla had known standing up to Steven would make him stop speaking to her, for real, she would've done it years ago.

He'd promised his heart, but all she got was an illusion and heartbreak. Her whole family and the friends she used to have, long ago, thought her marriage was perfect. Steven worked as an executive in the largest bank in town. He was handsome and kept his physique as taut as it had been throughout their college days. He demanded she not work, despite the master's degree she'd earned right alongside his MBA, for which she graduated *summa cum laude*, to his barely 2.0 GPA.

Their home was well-appointed and looked like a model home, situated on two acres in a gated community. They both drove newer model cars that Steven insisted on leasing and trading in every two years. Just when she got used to the bells and whistles on one, it was gone, replaced by a newer model.

She knew Steven wanted to trade her in for a newer model too, but she never gave him just cause. She kept their home spotless, working without the maid Steven claimed they didn't need to help her cover the four thousand square feet. Layla was witty and entertained his clients and bosses and colleagues whenever he wanted, in just the ways he liked, showing off their "opulent-but-we're-just-regular-people" lifestyle he lived for. Their two children were well-behaved—enough—at least, from Steven's standpoint, because he never spent any time with them. He just knew they were cute and involved in the "right" kinds of activities. Again, Layla shuttled them to and from all the things he wanted them to do.

Their kids were cute and smart...but they were also selfish and entitled. They were a handful, and Layla struggled to instill good values into them so they'd turn out to be productive citizens of society and not ungrateful people like their father. Steven decided she didn't need any help with the kids, though. Layla was a stay-at-home mother and wife, and he wanted her to be tied to all things domestic. Alone.

None of her efforts counted, though she kept up with everything on her own. Steven never insulted her outright because he didn't have any basis. He told other people she didn't want for anything. Behind closed doors, she had to ask permission to spend money on every little thing and risked Steven deciding she didn't need it and him telling her she couldn't have it. She usually acquiesced, not wanting to give him the excuse to cross the line from emotionally and financially abusive to the physically abusive he seemed closer to the longer they were married.

By the time she saw the post for film festival presentations in Europe, she would've taken any avenue that would get her out of the house for a couple of weeks, away from her ugly husband and terrible kids. Just the thought of a ten-hour flight to Germany was a respite from her picture-perfect trappings that only amounted to pretty bondage.

"What are you telling me about this for? Why should I care?" Steven's eyes lowered to slits as he thrust the presentation acceptance letter toward her.

She couldn't allow him to ruin her excitement. He might not see her worth, but the film festival organizers had seen value in her presentation topic.

"I proposed a talk, and the festival accepted it." She decided to tell him all the news in one go. "I've already booked my flight, and I leave next week. I'll be gone for ten days. I'll leave the kids' schedules for you, and everything will be fine."

He balled up the paper. "You spent my money on this nonsense, and now you're telling me you're just going to leave your kids? Me?" He folded his arms. "You're not going. I'm going to cancel everything and put the money back."

Layla shook her head. "I didn't take any money from your account. This is fully paid."

His dark brown complexion turned an ashen purple before he blustered toward her.

"So now you're sneaking money and hiding it from me?" He reached out to grab her, and she sidestepped him.

"No."

He stood, frozen in his anger. She could feel the waves of anger bubbling from him. She stood her ground. Once he spun on his heel and stalked away from her, she let out the breath she'd been holding.

She was going. And he couldn't stop her.

Steven didn't speak to her at all for the entire week before she left. Layla was happier than she had been in a long time. She spent her days making sure the kids' lunches and school clothes were in order.

She also took time to daydream about the hotel room she'd booked. The festival organizers had sent links to several chain hotels in the area. Layla didn't want what might be her only escape for years to be spent in a huge, sterile hotel. She'd scoured the travel sites until she found a cute little boutique hotel that wasn't especially far from the festival site.

A cobbled walkway led to large, Victorian-facing, floor-to-ceiling windows shining out of the online pictures. Layla pored over the additional pictures that showcased three courtyards, staircase nooks, and a delicate wrought iron spiral staircase. She could have breakfast at the hotel every morning. Truth be told, she was sold from the moment she saw the first picture. It drew her into its image, enveloping her in a warm embrace she could feel through the computer screen.

She couldn't pull the images up after she made her reservation, so she relied on her memory of them, which didn't let her down when she had to shout at her taxi driver to stop as he passed the hotel.

"Here!" She didn't speak German, but the driver understood her English well and followed her command. He turned to face her and gestured toward the street with his hand.

"Here?"

"Yes!" She recognized the hotel from the images emblazoned on her memory. "This is it."

The driver looked around and finally shook his head. With a heavy sigh, he got out of the car and walked around to help her unload her suitcase from the trunk.

She grabbed it when he made no motion to do so for her and headed up the walkway. "Thank you!" She'd still leave him a tip, even though he hadn't made any move to help her take her bag at least up to the steps.

It wasn't too much for her to do herself, not with all the excitement thrumming through her. She only had to make it to ring the front doorbell for entry before the woman who answered rolled her bag into the foyer. After the sounds of their movements died down, Layla heard a faint whispering–*hissing?* It almost sounded like a cat, padding along, brushing a full coat against the wall as it traveled. She hoped it was a cat that she'd get to meet while she was there. Steven detested animals and adamantly refused to allow them to have a pet of any kind, even when she used the kids as an excuse.

The woman's brown eyes sparkled with a youthfulness her slick, thick, gray hair belied. "You must be Layla. Checking in?"

"Yes. Thank you." Layla removed her scarf and coat. The foyer was cozy and warmed to a comfortable temperature, much better than the blustery, wet wind outside the doors.

She followed the woman to a small alcove that served as the

hotel's check-in desk. Old photographs dotted the walls, and Layla marveled at the floral-patterned wallpaper behind them.

"This is a unique pattern. Beautiful." She reached out to touch it but thought better of it. She didn't want to be rude to her hostess.

"Yes. It's original to the building. This used to be a private residence, built right after the war." She produced a metal key attached to a colorful key fob. "I'll give you our biggest room, yeah? Follow me, please."

Layla did as she was instructed and rolled her suitcase behind her, slowly hoisting it down each step to the lower level. More rustling followed them, echoing above her in the spiral stairway. She watched her step and her suitcase carefully, not wanting to injure any furry new friends. A place that beautiful would have more than one cat. She was sure of it. And it made her smile.

"I hope it's okay. The room is on our lower level." The older woman looked to Layla, seemingly for agreement.

Layla didn't feel any ill will coming from the woman, and she was sure she hadn't placed her in the basement because she was a Black woman. She nodded to her host. "It's fine."

Walking through the heavy wooden door the other woman held open for her made her head spin. "It's more than fine. This is…breathtaking!"

The woman smiled. "Yes. I told you I'll give you the big room."

The room was much larger than Layla knew hotel rooms in Europe tended to be. Hardwood floors covered with colorful throw rugs welcomed her inside. One wall, covered with a different floral pattern of black outlines with yellow shadowing, held Layla entranced. This time, she did touch it, unable to resist the urge.

She hadn't expected the intricate pattern to have been deeply embossed into the paper. Layla gasped and jerked her hand back when the deep grooves undulated beneath her fingertips.

"…the bathroom is okay?"

Layla shook her head. There was no movement in the wallpaper. She was jet-lagged, and the flowers and vines made her dizzy, giving the impression of movement. She chalked up feeling the movement to being tired.

Laya headed toward the second, smaller room where the hostess called her from. Contemporary, metallic tile created a trim through the middle of earth colored ceramic tile. A stand-alone rain shower called to her, and she sighed aloud.

The other woman smiled. "Yes. It's nice?"

"It's perfect."

"I'll leave you to get settled." Before she left the room, the woman turned in the doorway. "I'm Berta. If you need anything, just call. And the internet says we have breakfast every morning, but we also have tea in the afternoons and dinner at night, for special guests." She winked at Layla. "I hope you'll join us this evening, up on the third floor."

Layla smiled. "That's very nice of you. After I have a good shower, I'd love to."

She had been afraid the shower would render her exhausted after her travels, but instead, she was re-energized. And she was starved. The echo of the gentle water stream from her completed shower resounded in her head, its soothing, whispery rhythm following her into the bedroom.

Berta hadn't specified exactly where on the third floor the food was being served, but she hoped the hotel was easy to navigate. She soon found that the floors each held about six rooms, each, with hers being the only guest room on the bottom floor.

The first floor, where the check-in was located, had five additional rooms, each indicated by a number sign or a door décor item. The second floor held six rooms, situated close to each other, connecting. She paused to catch her breath on the landing on the second floor, hoping for a glimpse of one of the felines she still heard swishing about covertly.

The third floor held only a stairwell alcove with two sitting chairs and a tea table and two large, wooden doors. When Layla saw the hand sanitizer on the table outside the doors and the slip of paper indicating breakfast hours, she figured she'd made it to the right place.

"Hello?" She eased one side of the doors open slowly.

"Hello! Come on in, Mrs. Burton."

Layla opened the door to face four women already seated with Berta at the largest of the tables in the room. "Oh, Layla is fine." She didn't want to be reminded of the life she'd have to return to all too soon. While she was there, she was just Layla.

"Layla, it is. Come. Sit. Join us."

Each of the women sat in front of a steaming mug and an empty plate. Berta noticed her looking at the settings and spoke up.

"We didn't want to start without you. We'll eat now. You go first."

"Thank you." Layla turned her attention to the chafing dishes along the sides of the counters. Delicious smells wafted through the air, reminding her of how hungry she was. She decided on schnitzel and potatoes and made herself a salad. She waited until her hostesses had also filled their plates before she began to eat.

As she waited, Layla studied the wallpaper in the dining space. Bold red, orange, and yellow flowers tangled with bright green stems without leaves. The longer she watched, the more animated the design became, finally dancing in place with shimmery, swaying movements.

The changing pattern escalated Layla's hunger. She was ravenous. She ate heartily, indulging her curiosity at what the pattern would swirl into each moment, as she half engaged in the dinner table conversation.

The other women kept a lively spirit going with their banter about various things. Berta asked one about the quilt she was working on. The woman to Layla's left asked the others about the types of vegetables they'd plant in the grounds garden for spring. They allowed Layla to finish eating before turning their attention to her.

"So. What brings you to Berlin?"

Layla gripped the mug of tea she'd poured herself. "I'm giving a talk at a film festival."

"Oh, that sounds like fun! So you're a scholar?"

"Not really. I haven't done anything like this since grad school. But…" her voice trailed off as unexpected tears stung her eyes. She needed a hug.

"Are the resident cats here shy?"

"Cats?"

"Yes. I keep hearing them in the hallways, but I haven't seen them. Do they stay to themselves?" She wanted to change the subject, to indulge in comforting talk of anything other than the anxiety and anger burning in her chest. The wallpaper danced to the thrumming beat of her increasing heart rate.

One woman patted her hand and ignored her question. "It's okay, dear. We're glad you're here. It's just us ladies, around a table, sharing a meal, good tea, and a little chit chat."

Layla swiped at her eyes. "Thank you. I'm just glad to be away from home."

The women nodded.

"Things between my husband and I are terrible. My kids are horrible. I wanted to get away from them." She placed her face in her hands and mumbled, "I don't even miss them."

Berta reached over and patted her shoulder. "There, now, dear. It's really okay. We all understand exactly how you feel. That's why we live here and not where we used to."

Layla sniffed. "Really?"

"Really. After my husband died, I was so glad to be free of him, I came straight here and never looked back."

Another woman began to speak in broken English. "My husband and kids, gone. I stay here now. With my sisters."

All the women nodded.

"I'm glad I'm not the only one trying to escape." Layla smiled.

"No, you aren't."

She chatted with the women for a few more minutes and headed to bed, belly full of food and heart full of relief and kinship with the older women she'd bonded with. The little hotel felt like home.

Layla spent the next day working on her presentation. She skipped all the hotel sponsored meals, and by the time she looked up from her slides, the sun had gone down. Unsure whether or not dinner would be available that late, she instead logged onto a food delivery app, happy those things translated well across country boundaries.

She headed up the stairs, studying the detail in the spiral railing, when the time for her food delivery arrived. Still not having caught sight of any cats, she wondered briefly if the movements and increased rustling were made by something other than cats. Layla had no idea what sorts of pests might be native to that part of town. She'd have to ask again. There was something in the hotel sounding…restless, reflecting her steadily increasing anxiety.

Layla stood at the door of the hotel, alone in the dark foyer. She wondered what the other women were doing and resolved to have breakfast with them the next morning before she headed to the film festival.

A man in a thin jacket caught her eye, walking on the street in front of the hotel, carrying a small cooler. She stepped outside the door. "Hello!" she called. He didn't seem to hear her. She ran to the street, calling after him.

Suddenly, he turned around, startled to see her.

"Food delivery for Burton?" she asked.

"Yes. I was looking for your address. Sorry."

She gestured over her shoulder. "It's right there. No worries. I can carry the stuff back."

The man hesitated, continuing to look around.

"Don't worry, I think the addresses here are a little different from what I'm used to. I won't give you a low rating or take away your tip."

The man moved faster, handing her the food items and turning around swiftly, headed back to the opening to the little cul-de-sac alleyway, where Layla could see a car parked on the main street.

She returned to the warmth of the little hotel, closing the outside door firmly behind her to make sure it locked. Voices wafted to her in the hallway, masculine and feminine. Soft giggles made their way to the stairway and hung in the air. She was happy someone was enjoying spending time with their man.

Layla would never be that happy with Steven. She had some tough choices to make when she got back home.

If she went back home.

The thought came, unbidden, as she eased the door to her room open and went inside. Did she have to go back home? There would be a visa to attend to, and she'd have to figure out how to change her citizenship if she wanted to stay there. Maybe she could work at the hotel in exchange for somewhere to live and a small income. She would only have to worry about herself, so she wouldn't need much.

Did she want to stay there? Or was she just having these feelings about the women who made her feel welcome in a way she hadn't felt in any other space since well before she got married? Did she just want to escape home, and could do that more easily in a whole other country where Steven was unlikely to come and track her down in?

She fell asleep into warm dreams of black flowers and yellow shadows caressing her, filling her with energy. Surrounding her. Embracing her.

Layla went straight back to the hotel after her presentation. The organizers were nice, and the audience applauded her insights and analysis of the depiction of motherhood in horror films. She even had the chance to talk to a high-level academic who was visiting from a university in the UK afterward, about an open position as a visiting scholar.

Layla relished in the attention; however, all she wanted was to get back to her new friends and tell them all about her morning. She rushed from the taxi and emerged further down the alleyway when he passed the hotel up.

"Hello, sister Layla! We missed you yesterday." Berta smiled at her as she pressed a cup of tea into her hands.

"We figured you were busy with your work, so we didn't want to bother you."

"How did it go?"

Layla filled the air with her description of her presentation and the audience response. Her sisters clapped for her when she was done.

"We're so happy for you!"

She took in their genuine well-wishes and began to cry. Embarrassed, she tried to stand up and leave the table. Gentle hands pressed her back down into her seat.

"You don't have to be ashamed in front of us. We understand."

"I don't think you possibly could. My marriage is over. It has been for years. I don't like my kids very much. I really…I think I hate my husband."

"You do." Berta sipped from her own mug.

"I do." Layla hissed, remotely aware that the smiling woman knew the vehemence wasn't directed at her. The depth of her hate for Steven seared her soul, and now that she acknowledged it, she could only give it its reign.

Berta encouraged her anger.

"How much do you hate him?"

Layla felt the burning heat welling up inside her chest. "I hate him so much. I wish he would disappear."

"Disappear? Is that what you really wish?"

"No. I wish I could…just…tear him apart, ripping his appendages off. I want to drink from his throat and bleed him out while I chew on his heart. I…want him to suffer."

"He will."

"And I want to send his kids to hell with him."

"You can."

Layla stood up from the table, fury clouding her eyes.

"Why don't you take a walk outside for a little bit?"

Her hands trembled with her fury. She trained her eyes on the aggressively undulating wallpaper, seeking solace but finding more violent encouragement. "Yes."

She walked slowly down the spiral staircase, watching the patterns in the wallpaper along the rail dance happily around her. When she arrived at the door at the end of the foyer, she saw a taxi drive past with the face of her daughter pressed against the window. Sure she was still reeling from the intensity of emotions, she ran outside to the sidewalk. The taxi turned around and came back towards her.

Steven got out of the taxi, cursing her. "Where is that damned hotel you traipsed off to?"

"What are you doing here? Did you… Did you pull the kids out of school to bring them here?"

"Well, when their selfish bitch of a mother abandons them, and me, what else am I supposed to do?" He yelled at the taxi driver. "Get our stuff, man!"

The kids scrambled from the car, wrapping themselves around her legs.

"Mommy, why did you leave us?"

"Mommy, he touched me."

"Mommy, Daddy said he's leaving us here with you."

"Mommy."

"Mommy."

"Mommy."

"Where is this room of yours? It better be big enough for them. I'm leaving for home in the morning."

Layla walked past Steven and headed back to the hotel. She could hear him mumbling behind her.

When she got to the top of the stairs to the double doors, he and the kids stood on the sidewalk, silent for the first time since they'd arrived moments before.

"The hell did this place come from?"

"Mommy, are you magic?"

Her family followed her down the foyer, towards the spiral staircase. Berta stood in the doorway of the check-in alcove. She nodded her head. Layla nodded in return.

Her other sisters stood outside various doors along the hallway and bent over the staircase. They nodded. Layla nodded back.

She arrived at her room and held the door open for her family.

Steven threw his overnight bag onto the floor and crossed to press Layla up against the wallpapered wall.

"If you ever pull this kind of shit again, I'll choke the shit out of you. Got it?" His breath was hot on her face, wet and musky.

"No. Do you got it?" Layla grabbed his protruding lips and snatched them from his face, closing her eyes in ecstasy at the wet sounds of torn skin and Steven's surprised gurgle. He didn't have time to scream before she took the ripped flesh and drilled two holes into his forehead with her newly sharpened thumbs and pushed the pieces into them. Elongated, floral fingers wrapped around the back of his head, holding him in place.

She cackled when the resistance deep inside the holes gave way to the intrusion with satisfying moist sounds.

Layla spun him around and threw him against the wall, where black flowers danced to life. Florets continued to spin from her fingertips, and thick tendrils wrapped themselves around his throat. Yellow shadows ripped at his skin, drawing blood wherever they touched. She relished the shades of red blending with the yellow and black pattern, creating a new variation that delighted her.

Steven futilely tried to grab at her appendages around his throat with one hand and swatted at his forehead with the other. His screams weakly emerged as croaks as gushing blood ran down over his teeth and into his mouth.

She and the wallpaper pressed him deeper into the wall as Layla sliced his ears off, one at a time, and stuffed them into his mouth, forcing his bloodied teeth open. "You loved controlling me, breaking me down, and making me small. Look at me now! Larger than your pathetic little life." She stuck her chest out, a crown of entangled flowers emerging from atop her head, settling into a headpiece that instantly made her two feet taller.

"I'm done with this. With you. Do you know how long I've wanted to just kill you to shut you up?" Layla laughed again, triumphant, joyous tears spilling down her cheeks.

She stabbed at his torso with new sprouts from her body, sliding the razor-sharp branches upwards until she reached his chest cavity. She reached in and impaled his still beating heart. "I no longer want your heart. Except to feast on it."

Layla took a bite from the organ, and blood spewed from the flesh, dribbling down her chin, carrying tiny bits of sinewy muscle that escaped her lips. Ever-emerging vines slithered across the stream, smearing it as they suckled at the nourishment. She chewed slowly, making sure she stayed within his pained gaze, forcing him to watch her actions. She stared into his eyes until they became unfocused, drained of consciousness.

She stopped chewing when she heard the faint splattering of liquid on the hardwood floor. The sound hadn't come from Steven's body. It was in another part of the room. She then remembered her children were there. Her tendrils carried her to where they stood, frozen in place. Her son had wet himself. Her daughter stared at her in awe, mesmerized, a hesitant smile on her face—though she looked poised to flee as their mother came closer to them.

Layla didn't really want to kill her children.

They hadn't done anything wrong. She would have to work with her son. But her baby girl already carried the heart and understanding of a fellow warrior. Without the influence of their father, they would be reared into a goddess and a man worthy of being married to a powerful woman. Their future was bright, and Layla was proud that they would have the upbringing they deserved, with a strong mother who could love them fully in her emancipation, rather than a shell of a woman bound by the shackles of abuse.

"I won't hurt you, my babies. She tilted her head in their direction. "I love you both. Always. Your father had to go. He was a terrible person, and he held us all in bondage. We're free now, and we'll be happy."

Her sisters appeared from the walls surrounding her.

"Yes, good decision, sister. The kids shouldn't die."

"No, we will spare them. They can be useful members of our household."

"Finish your meal. We'll get the little ones cleaned up and make them some dinner." Berta held her hand out to the children. Layla's daughter immediately grabbed the older woman's hand, her fascinated concentration on her mother broken.

Anya motioned to her brother. "Come on, Stevie. You heard Mommy. We're free. We'll all be happy."

Her little brother grasped her hand, his tears halted, and followed her and Berta out of the room.

"He was never here. No one even knows we're here. Dispose of him to your heart's desire."

Layla resumed chewing, in silence, reveling in the dancing flowers on the wallpaper that mimicked their intricate pattern on her body.

FOURTEEN
NO TRICKS, ONLY TREATS

Nobody ever went trick-or-treating in their housing projects.

Ally used to ask Titi if they could go when she was younger. Titi always said no. Said it was stupid to send kids begging for candy that would rot their teeth and make them bounce around, tearing up stuff.

Titi thought a lot of things were stupid—mostly, anything Ally asked to do. When Ally asked if they could visit her mother's grave, Titi replied, "Why? She's dead. She won't know we're there."

When Ally asked for new clothes as she'd outgrown her old ones years past, Titi replied, "No. You don't need new clothes."

Ally had tried one last time to get her aunt to buy her clothes that fit properly. "Please, Titi, the kids at school are mean to me about my raggedy clothes. And the teachers ask me so many questions."

Titi narrowed her eyes when Ally mentioned the teachers. She looked so like Ally's mother, Titi's sister. But she was nothing like the sweet woman who had left her daughter all too soon.

"Then you ain't going back to school. I'm checking you out of there tomorrow."

Leaving school completely wasn't what Ally had in mind, but at least she didn't have to suffer any more bullying. Not at school, anyway.

She'd learned to ignore the slaps and shoves. The only part that still hurt was when Titi withheld food from Ally, which was quite often. She was always hungry once she couldn't eat at school anymore.

Ally tiptoed over to the single window in her bedroom. She stealthily peeked through the middle slit to make sure Titi wasn't downstairs on the tiny square slab of concrete that served as their patio. Not seeing the telltale flicker of Titi's cigarette, Ally fully looked out.

She watched a small child and their mother walk up to the porch of an apartment across the way. The child moved with plodding steps, determined yet wobbly.

The mother stood at the end of the walkway in the light of the full moon. The woman's longing was palpable as it crawled across the grass and pavement, slipped along the side of Ally's building, and entreated Ally to continue watching.

The mother's body visibly deflated when the child began to move away from the door that never opened, back toward her.

Ally resisted the urge to slide away from the window, out of sight in the wake of the pair's sadness. Instead, she nodded when her eyes met theirs.

She had to get down to the door before Titi did to make sure the child got the one piece of candy Ally could offer.

Ally went to her closet and pulled down a contraband candy bar she had been hiding for over a month. The stolen snack was Ally's only defense against starvation. But giving it to the child would make Ally feel better than a ceasing of her hunger pangs.

She eased her bedroom door open and tried to see where Titi was. When she didn't see or hear her, she ran down the stairs as fast as she could.

"What the hell is wrong with you?" Titi's voice startled Ally, and she tripped, falling next to the door.

"I was just..." Ally stammered, instinctively bringing her arms up in their usual position, protecting her head from Titi's frequent blows.

"Don't open that door!"

Titi cursed as the door banged open, turning her head to follow Ally's gaze to the two figures that stood in their front doorway.

"Get out of my house!"

"No tricks, only treats."

The voice was not the voice of a child.

Titi swung out again, her arm suddenly freezing. Her body also stilled.

"I...I'm sorry," Ally stood. She held the candy bar towards the child. A tiny hand reached out to take it. Ally's gaze met eyes with no whites, black orbs nestled into brown skin, and a baby's plump face.

"Thank you. Thank you. Thank you." The mother uttered the phrase over and over again in a tune similar to the sing-song cadence the child spoke in.

"You are kind, child."

Ally didn't bristle at the word. This was no child.

"Yes," the person continued. "You are a kind child who does not deserve to live the way you do. This one" —a chubby hand motioned towards Titi— "is of the darkest soul."

The hand flicked out, and Titi's arms snapped, blood spraying from the fracture. Another flick, and Titi bent over backward with a wet, grinding sound.

Ally's widened gaze moved between Titi's breaking body, the child inflicting the breaks, and the woman who had dropped to her knees on the stoop, tears streaming thickly down her face.

"She deserves to die a painful death." Titi's head followed the motion of the child's arm, spinning on her neck.

"But what will happen to me? I.... I'm only sixteen."

"Do not worry. I will leave you with a more suitable caregiver."

The child reached down and grabbed the sides of its mother's head. Expecting more carnage, Ally winced, then gasped as a shadowy haze developed at the fingertips and swirled around.

The tiny hands guided the haze into Titi's fallen form. Broken bones snapped into place. "Off you go, your penance done. Live this second life in service to this child as you have served me."

Titi's eyes opened, and she slowly moved her repaired limbs.

"And you, foul one, begin your penance now. We will travel far and wide to find one more sinister than you." One last flick of the child-like wrists captured a second transparent form bearing the terrified visage of Titi before pressing it into the other body on the floor.

Ally whimpered as the body moved awkwardly, stiffly, defiance shining in the eyes.

"Do not think you can escape. We travel the earth every All Hallows' Eve to continue our search. Come."

The small body led the woman out of the apartment. A soft voice pulled Ally's gaze away from where the new pair faded into the moonlight.

"Let me clean up this mess and fix you something to eat."

Ally studied the female form for any remnants of her aunt. "Do you think we could go trick-or-treating for a little while, first?" She figured it wouldn't hurt to ask.

Her new aunt smiled at her, genuine pleasure showing through. "Of course. Anything you want. It'll be a wonderful treat."

FIFTEEN
THE PREYING FAMILY

Day One
Umoja: Unity

Tabitha

"I wanna get the kinara and the candles, Mama. Please, Mama. I'm a big girl. I can help now. I'm six years old." The beads at the ends of Lizzie's braids rattled, bouncing around her jumping body.

Tabitha placed her hand on Lizzie's shoulder to still her. "We have to wait until Daddy gets home before we can start." She smoothed Lizzie's now still head with a loving caress.

Chelsea sucked her teeth. "We always have to wait for him before we can do fun stuff."

Tabitha pinned her older daughter with a weak but stern gaze. "Watch your mouth. Just because you're nineteen doesn't mean you can be disrespectful like that. Your father works hard to take care of us, so wait we must."

"Dad always comes home the day after Christmas," Lance stated.

Chelsea rolled her eyes at him.

Lizzie began to jump up and down again. Tabitha released a sigh.

"Hey, lil bit, why don't you come help me carry the candles from the pantry?" Thaddeus offered his long-suffering mother a brief reprieve from the unrelenting energy of their younger sister.

Lizzie ran over to her older brother and loudly proclaimed, "I know which ones! One black, three green, and three red. See?"

"Did you get everything ready for tomorrow morning, Gabriel?" Tabitha quizzed her youngest son. They didn't stay babies for long.

He answered in the sonorous instrument his voice had become over the past year. "Yes, ma'am."

The front door opened, halting their conversation. Her husband's form entered. She walked as quickly as she could to collapse into his arms.

"My beloved." John hugged his wife, inhaling the scent of the coconut oil moisturizing her long locks. "Did I miss anything?"

"Chelsea was trying to rush us along without you," Lance offered.

"Is that so?" John walked to his daughter. "Were you trying to count your old man out?"

The thick veneer of teen angst Chelsea wore like a second skin melted off, and she hugged her father. "No...it just gets hard to wait all the time."

"But wait, we must," Lizzie yelled, re-entering the room, holding the kinara carefully with both hands. Everyone laughed.

Gabriel unfolded the mkeka and placed it gently across the table. Lance helped Lizzie set the kinara down in the middle of the cloth. Thaddeus followed with the candles, which he also placed on the cloth.

Lizzie turned towards her parents. "Please, can I put the candles in? I promise I'll be really, really careful."

Tabitha looked to John, who nodded his head.

"Yes, you can arrange the candles," Tabitha said.

Lizzie climbed up into a chair and reverently placed each red candle on the left side of the kinara, and the green candles on the right side. Once she placed the larger, center black candle in the middle slot, Tabitha spoke again.

"I think Lizzie is old enough to light her own candle tonight. The first one, so there's no other fire."

"She's a big girl now. I'll help you, Lizzie."

John held the fire lighter in his large hand and placed it into Lizzie's palm. He then guided her hand towards the black candle. "Do you remember what to say on this first day?"

Lizzie screwed up her small face and then shouted, "Umoja. We are one family. United."

The family repeated her words, excited to start their holiday week.

Day Two
Kujichagulia:
Self-Determination

Gabriel

The next morning, John, Chelsea, Lance, and Thaddeus stood with Gabriel in their detached barn. They watched him as he worked to move the pail of blood from underneath the skinned carcass hanging from the rafters. He replaced the bucket with a large sheet of plastic. Then, he reached up to cut the rope holding the carcass. He tossed it over his shoulder, then onto the tarp.

The figure no longer resembled the developer who had come out for another attempt at coercing the family into selling their home to the company he worked for.

They watched, long into the morning, as Gabriel sliced the meat from the bones. He tossed the meat into one empty bucket and chunks of fat into another.

"This year, we make sausage to sell at the county fair. Thaddeus, take the blood to the back porch and put it in the ice chest. Chelsea, go prepare a fire pit to burn these bones. Dad, please start grinding this meat in the grinder. Lance, take these intestines and clean them for the casements." His family disbursed to follow his orders.

That night, it was Gabriel's turn to light the first red candle. "Kujichagulia. I am now a self-determined man, forging my own path, making my own decisions, in service to my family and tradition."

The family repeated his words, eager to get to bed early for an early start on the next day.

Day Three
Ujima:
Collective Work and Responsibility

Lance

The family worked all day the next day, making sausage. They ground seasonings to add to the meat mixture. They cut and stuffed casings. They took turns checking the smoker, making sure the temperature was perfect. Even Lizzie had an important job: She had to count the links and keep track of the numbers with her pink marker and fancy notebook.

At the end of the evening, Lance lit the first green candle. "Ujima. Through collective work and responsibility, we will provide for one another, always."

The family repeated after him, exhausted, but content.

Day Four
Ujamaa:
Cooperative Economics

Chelsea

. . .

The family rested through the next day. When the sun set, Chelsea brought a small safe into the dining room and emptied it on the table. Thick stacks of bills fell from it.

"How are you doing, Chelsea?" Her mother fixed her with a concerned gaze. The girl said she was fine since the assault by that nasty Turner boy, but Tabitha wanted to be sure. He had only gotten so far before Chelsea had bitten his tongue and run from him.

"I'm fine, Mama. Really. Especially since we have this $25,000 that stupid boy was stealing from his father's store."

"That damned knucklehead was lucky you and Lance got to him before I did." John's low voice held menace his family rarely heard.

"Oh, he was unlucky, Daddy. But the gators in the creek got a fortune in good meat."

Chelsea lit the second red candle. "Ujamaa. Cooperative economics, as restitution from trespassers, will fund our family. Always."

Her family emphatically repeated her words.

Day Five
Nia: Purpose

Tabitha

"We must keep the family at seven, until the kids start building their own families."

Tabitha mumbled the words over and over as she tilled the soil of the flowerbed surrounding their humble home with her bare hands. She unearthed a small skull, and tears filled her eyes. She placed a tender kiss onto the bone and dug deeply with her other hand to re-bury it. She felt other small bones, just at the tips of her fingers, but she didn't linger over her extra babies that day. There would be no more babies for her.

That night, she lit the second green candle. "Nia. With purpose, I will forever keep my family in favor with the ancestors."

The family echoed her, certain in their knowledge that they continued to live in favor because of her steadfast dedication.

Day Six
Kuumba: Creativity

Thaddeus

"I'm up to nine on the number of hikers I've dispatched of." Thaddeus made his announcement over dinner the sixth night.

Gabriel congratulated his brother. "Good! Trampling all through our land, all disrespectful and stuff."

"You make sure they won't be found or looked for?" John eyed his oldest son.

"Yes, sir. I put four of them in those flimsy little cracker boxes they're building a few miles down. Made it look like the developer man did it and then ditched. The other six, I buried in the concrete of the wet foundations, where they didn't have any security cameras. If they find them, they'll think he did them in, too."

Tabitha's eyes lit up. "My son. The creative soul."

Later, Thaddeus lit the third red candle. "Kuumba. With creativity, I will always protect and provide for my family."

His family repeated his sentiments.

Day Seven
Imani: Faith

Tabitha

The seventh day waned with the somber Winston family preparing for the last night of their festivities. After dinner, John lit the last green candle.

"Imani. Through unwavering faith in our traditions, our family will continue in favor."

Everyone repeated the intonation.

Tabitha remained in silence. Before the next holiday season, they had to make a hard decision. She would tell John about their predicament and ask for his guidance in finding a solution. If she expired before this time next year, they'd be one less of their required seven. If by some miracle she survived this pregnancy and birthed the babe, they'd be one over. There was no guarantee she would survive terminating the babe, either. They both could expire.

If it came down to it, she would sacrifice herself and the babe and get John to press Thaddeus to marry before the holidays. John would not hesitate to kill her for their family.

Imani. Faith.

IMPORTANT THINGS

Mama would have had a fit if she had known I let those kids call me out of my name.

"Close your mouth, C.C."

I couldn't hold back my glee at all the wonders my travels offered, how big the planes were—how the water on Long Beach was actually blue rather than the sickly brown of our closest Galveston beaches in the Gulf.

Those kids were cool and jaded about everything. Where I was in awe, they shrugged their shoulders.

"It's just water."

"Heathrow offers way better amenities than this little airport."

"The plane my family took to Japan was bigger than all of these."

I decided not to blame them for all they thought they knew. I saw early on they didn't know critical things like I did. None of them uttered respectful requests for the protection of the ancestors before the plane rose in the air. Nor did they give thanks for the steadying of the pilot's hands upon our landing.

The Christmas tree in the fancy hotel lobby stood almost as high as the trees in my inner-city neighborhood and glittered like a priceless treasure. Lush greenery adorned in gold and silver ornaments sparkled throughout the halls. There was even pristine fake snow to make up for the fact it didn't snow in Southern California.

That was no matter to me. I never saw snow at home, either, so the design didn't offend. My mouth fell open, as it seemed to be destined for the remainder of my journey, and I could feel my eyes filling with tears of gratitude at the chance to spend part of my Christmas holiday in that beautiful space.

The kids who had decided they would allow me to hang out with them at the airport and on the way to the hotel had come from all over the country—but none from Texas, like me. They seemed so polished. So…citified.

So rude.

I had told them several times my name was Lizabeth, and they had ignored me every time. They found my gapped teeth "charming" and my heavy Southern accent "cute," so they re-christened me C.C. for Country Cute. I was only just vested enough in maintaining their company so I wouldn't be completely alone that I didn't argue against the moniker, but only answered to it when they shortened it to the initials.

"Never forget who you are and where you come from," Mama always said. She had repeated this mantra as she pulled the rusted coffee can from deep inside her closet and unfolded a few wrinkled bills to hand me for my trip.

"Mama, I don't have to go." My high school guidance counselor had accosted me in the hallway at school earlier in November and demanded to know why she had not seen me in her office for college plans yet.

"I'm not sure I'm going to college," I had truthfully admitted as the stern lady herded me toward her office.

"With these grades? Yes, you most definitely are going to college." She had barely slid me into the second chair in the small room before she continued. "What do you want to be when you grow up?"

I thought of the long line of healers I came from—the way my

Granny used to be able to diagnose any sickness anyone anywhere had and offer a spot-on cure with just a glance and a listen.

"Umm. Maybe a doctor or something?" I mumbled these words, knowing there was no way my family could afford college, much less medical school.

The counselor beamed. "Yes! That's a great choice. As a matter of fact, there's an all-paid biomedical symposium being sponsored by Meharry Medical College for potential students next month. Attendees will be given priority scholarship consideration. You're going." Her fingers flew across her keyboard until her printer roared to life.

"I don't know if my Mama will let me go…"

She waved my words away and pressed the papers into my hand. She took another sheet from her desk and signed it with a flourish.

"This is an all expense paid trip. All the way to California! Give your mother this paperwork and have her sign. If she has any questions, have her call me."

I waited until I left her office and got around the corner to stuff the sheets way down deep into my backpack.

I forgot about them until Mama asked me about them a couple of days later.

"What is this about?"

"I. Ummm. Mrs. Leonard said this is a scholarship opportunity for medical students. And. Ummm…"

Her eyes went from excited to moist. "Were you not going to tell me about it?"

I never lied to my Mama. "I wasn't. I don't have to go. We don't have money like that, and I'm probably not even going to college."

She took my hands into her large, tough ones. I looked at the shiny red polish that was her signature color, the only concession she gave to frivolity.

"Listen, my Lizabeth. You're the smartest person I've ever known. You have to go to college. Don't you worry about paying for it. Your old mama got tricks up her sleeve you wouldn't know nothing about." And that was that.

She borrowed a suitcase from her employer and helped me pack. "Here's some new underwear and a couple of pairs of pantyhose." She held up the small, ornate box I had only ever seen her use a couple of times when our home altar was dismantled. "And don't forget to give thanks when you get into your hotel room. This is an opportunity that will change your life. I know it."

Even she and her second sight could not possibly have known how much truth was in her statement.

I tried to surreptitiously slide an orange and a handful of nuts from the ornate bowl on the desk to put into my coat pocket, even though the front desk clerk had told us to help ourselves.

The queen bee of the group, Mina, saw me. "You don't have to hide food here. They'll feed us." Her fake stage whisper singed my skin. Waves of giggles followed.

A hand settled on my shoulder, and I saw Chris reach over to grab an apple and a banana. "They put this here for us because they know people are hungry after travelling." I searched his face for signs of ridicule, thinking I was country and starving.

Finding none, I blushed. Christopher was cute. Tall. Clear skinned. And seemed to be the only one of the group that had any idea of how to be polite. All I could do in the wake of his kindness was whisper, "Yes."

He remained by my side as the sponsors escorted us into the fancy elevators and to our individual hotel rooms. We lingered just behind the last adult, and he slid the fruit into my shoulder bag. At my questioning glance, he shrugged his shoulders. "We might get hungry later. I'll come back for it."

I thought about his words the rest of the night as I unpacked my necessities. I did clear my head long enough to set up my altar and gently set the fruit and nuts on the delicate cloth Mama packed with it.

My earlier suspicions about my travel mates' ignorance to important things was confirmed as Sierra, the girl I was sharing my room with, interrogated me.

"Why are you piling fruit up like that? We'll get ants. And we don't need the food."

"What's that for? You a witch or something?"

I ignored her and continued to build my temporary altar the way Mama had taught me. The familiarity of creating an offering for the spirits helped settle the homesickness that bubbled up inside me when I realized I wouldn't be sleeping at home the next few nights.

I gave thanks for travelling grace and the opportunity that lay before me. I remained focused and poured salt along the doorway and the bathroom windowsill. There was not enough to place completely around the large window in the room, but I did what I could behind my offerings.

Sierra finally stopped her questions and threw her suitcase into a corner of the room. I heard her sneak out later after I'd gone to bed.

She didn't ask me to go along with her, and I didn't feel the least bit left out.

My early night in paid off quickly. The first day of the conference was exciting, but tiring. My brain buzzed with new information, and my stomach fluttered at Chris's closeness during every presentation. On breaks, he and I would talk about what we'd heard. He was really smart. All the kids were, and I had to realize I was in the space where I should be with the rest of them, intellectually. For the first time, I seriously entertained fantasies of attending college.

I could barely keep my eyes open when the sponsors said we could spend some free time in the places near the hotel. They gave us a curfew, and I was swept up in the gang as we headed towards the beach.

"It's strange to have Christmas without any snow," Mina chirped. "I couldn't even pack my Uggs."

"It's nice, though, to be able to enjoy walking around outside without freezing," one of the other boys chimed in.

"Yeah, I could never do this in Brooklyn," another added.

There was a slight chill in the air as the sun started its descent towards the waterline.

"It's time to eat. They said we have to get dinner on our own."

"Yeah. How about this ship restaurant?"

"That would be cool! I heard about this place."

I looked where Mina pointed. I mentally calculated how much money I had and whether or not I could afford to eat at the waterside restaurant that looked especially expensive. I hesitated.

Chris placed his hand in mine. "Let's go. I got you."

I couldn't think clearly when he was holding my hand like that. I knew I would have to pay my own way, but for that moment, I allowed myself to pretend I would let him take me on a date to that place.

For the second time in as many days, I stood in surprise at the reception podium. I had never been on a ship before and could hardly wrap my head around an elegant restaurant being on one. I felt the moniker of "country" most acutely as we stood in the opulent reception area of the restaurant we tumbled into. Rich, red velvet draping covered the floors and walls. Huge chandeliers almost blinded me when I looked directly at them.

Accent pieces that looked like real diamonds dotted the area, and I could hardly breathe for its beauty. We were having dinner on an actual ship! It was docked, but it still floated on the water. I tried to record every detail in my head to describe to Mama when I called her that night from my room. I didn't have a cell phone, and Chris offered to email me his pictures. I accepted his offer—but still wanted to commit all the finery to memory.

The waiter led us through the busy middle of the room. I could see the white tips of the cresting waves peeking out in the dark. I was happy he didn't seem to be taking us to the window seats. In the daytime, the water was beautiful, I was sure. In the dark, its energy felt magnetic. Hungry.

I was hungry, too. Once we finally arrived at a table in the back corner of one of the smaller rooms, I tried to read the menu, but it confused me. I had no idea how much anything cost. This was one of those fancy places I saw in movies where the food was served in courses, and they didn't list any prices.

The other kids had no such concerns. While I tried to steady my breathing and roundly calculate how far my limited cash would go on that menu, they ordered everything they thought looked good. I ordered a salad with salmon from the appetizer course and would just pass on the others. I couldn't figure out how to make any inquiry, especially when no one else, even Chris, was worried about it.

He pressed something delightful to my lips, and I melted. "How do you like that?"

I looked into his eyes and decided to use all the money Mama had given me, if I had to, just to enjoy this one evening.

We sat and laughed and talked and ate until the last diners sentenced to the purgatorial space with us had left.

Suddenly, Mina stood up, and the group followed her, unspeaking. "Come on, C.C.! You're too slow!"

I stammered. "What's going on…?"

Chris put his arm around me and practically carried me out the exit door and along the pier to the dark side of the nearest building. We stopped to catch our breath, and I turned to Chris. "What's happening? We didn't pay."

"You thought we were gonna pay for all that food? It tastes better when you don't."

"It wasn't even that good."

"Not worth whatever they wanted for it."

"But…"

Mina got right up in my face. Her brown eyes threw sparks. "What, are you going to go back and pay for all our food?" I wanted to lower my eyes, but held her gaze. "Right. I bet you can't. You better keep up and go with it."

They all broke into a run in the opposite direction, heading towards the hotel the long way around.

I tried my best to keep up because Mina was right. I was sure I didn't have enough money to pay for everything. And I didn't want to get in trouble. But stealing was wrong.

Chris seemed to read my mind. He stopped briefly and placed both hands on my shoulders. "It's just a little harmless dine and dash. They won't catch us. Just some fun—they can afford it." Then he led me into a trot where we caught up with the others.

We finally stopped at a part of the beach where we could see the dim twinkling of the ship's lights far off in the distance. The sound of the waves washing up on the shore should have been soothing, but it was not. We found large pieces of driftwood to sit on.

Everyone talked and laughed, and I remained silent, trying to figure out a solution. Chris had dropped my hand and rubbed his together, warding off the growing night chill.

One of the girls screamed—Sierra, I think—and the ocean ate the sound. I turned to where she had sat and only saw a vague whirl-wind of …something. Where her voice cut off, there were splatters of something damp. Another boy grunted, and right behind him stood a figure, luminescent in the darkness of the dimly lit shore. It held him up in arms that didn't look solid, but were able to turn his torso around to face the opposite direction of his feet, nonetheless.

The rest of us ran again, stumbling along the sand. My voice caught in my chest. Chris grabbed my hand again and pulled me with him. Squeals and ragged gurgles followed us until the sound of footsteps behind us dwindled away, set by set, until all we could hear were our own thudding footfalls.

I thought my lungs would burst as we tore through the back entrance to the hotel. We flew up the stairs, all the way to the fifth floor, where our rooms were. We only slowed down when we got to the hallway where our rooms were. We didn't want to alert any of the adults. Chris and I shared one last glance as he went into his room next door to mine. I pretty much figured out Sierra wouldn't be returning to our shared space that night.

I shut the door and went straight to the altar to pay penance. "I'm sorry, I'm sorry, I'm sorry…"

A guttural scream launched from the other side of the wall, and I fished out what I hoped were sufficient bills to pay for my meal. Muffled thuds continued over and over again. I jumped into the bed and pulled the covers over my head.

"I'm sorry, I'm sorry, I'm sorry…"

The temperature in the room dropped, and I kept the cover pulled up. I could smell seawater and that fresh scent of ice, like when you first open a freezer door and the cold wafts through. Soft whispers travelled around me, bringing the chill through the heavy blanket. I shivered. The sounds next door became wet, moist. Then stopped altogether.

"I'm sorry, I'm sorry, I'm sorry…"

I remained underneath the covers for long minutes, frozen, afraid to move until I realized I sat in complete silence and the room warmed up. I slid the blanket down and looked around. The space was still lit with the one light I had turned on when I came in.

Everything looked the same. I was alone. My suitcase remained on the bench. I looked at the door, still closed, with the line of salt intact. I turned to the window and noticed a swirling of the tail end of the line where I ran out of salt trailing out of the window. The bills and the orange were gone.

Mama would have had a fit if she had known what those kids and I had done that night. I never told her. I never told anyone. But she would have been proud that I never forgot who I was and where I was from, admitting my wrongdoing and paying penance to the spirits who we had disturbed on that ship.

I never forgot the important things in life.

SEVENTEEN
INHERITANCE

BRAM STOKER AWARDS® WINNER FOR
SUPERIOR ACHIEVEMENT IN SHORT FICTION

I bet you're wondering how a chick like me ended up covered in offal with my arm halfway down the throat of a slimy, rotted corpse.

It's a fair question. And it's my own damned fault.

Mama always said I was too big for my britches. Wanted champagne on a soda pop budget. Thought I was supposed to have the world when all most people got was a reasonably less torturous life than others.

She was right, even if I would never tell her that out loud—I liked my teeth just where they were, thank you very much. She never understood how I felt choked by the boundaries of our small Texas town, barely big enough to have a Walmart and a Dairy Queen. I grew up hating to change schools to only move from Chriten Elementary to Chriten Middle School to Chriten High School.

It didn't help that I hated school in the first place. Reading was difficult for me. Numbers never made any sense. I physically outgrew even my teachers by the time I was in the fifth grade, and my thick, kinky hair never uncoiled enough to flow down my shoulders like some of my classmates. The only reason I went to school was to get out of the house from up under Mama. And to at least listen to stories about places far away from the boredom I was sure would kill me before I made adulthood.

The only person who understood me was my Uncle Vick. Out of our huge family, centered in the same three neighboring towns for generations, he was the only one who had traveled away from home without doing so in the military or in prison. I lived for our chats, when there would be one kindred spirit to tell me it was okay to want more, to aim for better. To live life fully, even if that life was full of vices.

"Ain't nothing wrong with having goals outside this little shoe-box, Orlean," he often said to Mama, as he held the filtered cigarette that was a permanent fixture between his fingers or lips. He'd then suck his teeth and tell her I was nothing like her. When I was little, I always gasped when he said that, because the edge in his voice made those fighting words.

But Mama didn't seem offended. She'd just roll her eyes at him and then at me. "She need to make a goal to stay her ass in school and make better grades to get outta there. Then she can get married and have some kids and do what all the rest of us do around here: Live, love, and die, here in town. On our own land."

Uncle Vick would get the strangest look on his face every time she said that. I understood there was much more to the story than what either of them would probably ever tell me. From my eaves-dropping throughout childhood, a skill I perfected early, I learned Uncle Vick had paid off all the family homesteads with riches no one quite understood how he had. I don't think they particularly cared where the money came from as long as they could brag that our people owned something of great value that couldn't be easily erased.

I cared where the money came from. I wanted to learn everything about getting rich and moving to a huge mansion like where he lived. There had to be big fine houses well outside of Chriten, in bigger cities where things were happening. Where I could build a life big enough to fill me up through my empty insides.

Any time I could, I went to stay the weekend with Uncle Vick.

Mama put a halt to my frequent visits when I entered puberty, and I didn't fight her on it. He was nothing like the handsy uncles on other parts of our family tree, so I knew she wasn't worried about how my developing body could turn him into a predator. Whatever else she was thinking just wasn't important to me. She was just trying to clip my wings.

So, I called Uncle Vick to come get me and my overnight bag. Later, I simply waited until I got old enough to get my driver's license and drove myself. She didn't dare stop me once I showed her I was going to go, anyway.

Uncle Vick would walk me through the lush, multi-acre forest surrounding his well-kept Victorian home, telling me the history of each section. The two-story, fifteen-room house was much too large for my single uncle, who had never had a girl or boyfriend that any of us knew about, much less any children to fill the spaces. He seemed larger than life to me, taller even than me, and as wide as a linebacker. He took up plenty of space in the house and made it seem less empty when we were there.

"Do you ever want to have kids, Uncle?" I finally dared ask this burning question once I turned eighteen, set to graduate the upcoming spring. I figured I was grown enough to get into grown folks' business—especially since Mama wasn't there to remind me that I wasn't grown up yet.

I regretted it immediately when his face dropped, and his eyes went to some far-away spot across the tree line.

"I did use to think I wanted to. But that ain't my journey." He gestured at his homestead. "But all this has to go to someone who will care for it their whole life, like I will."

An unknown bubbling began in my chest, and I looked up at him. "I would do that, Uncle. I love this place. I love you."

He patted me on my shoulder. "I know you do. But you gotta do some more maturing. Live life a little bit. Learn how to harness our power. Then we can talk about it again later."

The unknown feeling made itself clear then: first of all, *what power?* Also, I had to make sure I inherited the kingdom so I'd have the money to live the kind of life I wanted. The life I needed.

He and I spent long walks through the family homestead, tossing rocks in the bordering swamp and meditating in front of numerous headstones in the on-site cemetery. I hadn't met most of the people buried there, and the dates went far back into the 1800s. A few of them had last names I didn't know to have been in our family line. Uncle Vick stayed before these the longest.

His reverence for life and beyond made him my favorite person in the world. Until he took a back seat to my first boyfriend, John Baldwin.

I couldn't think of much else once John started paying attention to me. I saw Uncle Vick less frequently. Hell, I saw myself less frequently then, too. I dressed how John wanted me to dress—acted the way he told me he wanted me to act. The butterflies he drove up inside my belly and between my legs told me to do everything just so, and he would always love me.

I truly believed that until the night I sneaked out of the house and went for a ride into the swamp with him. This part of the swamp was on the clear side of town from the waterways of my childhood. The trees there were louder, more sinister. I heard their clamor over the blood heating in my veins when John touched me.

And I couldn't say I didn't expect for him to want to touch me in more ways than I'd already allowed. There were no houses around that part of the swamp. The road wasn't even paved, so no one else would likely come driving along accidentally. The brush was too thick for casual walks.

He wanted to get me resoundingly alone, and I had allowed it.

What I hadn't allowed was the vicious attack he launched as soon as he put his car into park.

"John, wait!" I tried to pull his hands from underneath my skirt. "You're hurting me." I despised the simpering whine my voice had become as I fought him unsuccessfully. I'd never been afraid of anything, but in that moment, I was more afraid of John than I had ever been in my life.

His rough hands pinched me, and I felt bruises beginning without even looking at my skin. He tore my clothes and began to punch me, hard, all over.

"Don't play with me. You knew this was coming."

I hadn't known—not like that. And it wasn't going down *like that*. The more he hit me, the angrier I got. I clawed at him with renewed strength. Then I screamed louder than I knew I could, scaring myself with the power of rage behind the sound.

John halted his assault. His eyes grew wide, and blood began to pour from his ears. He choked and coughed up torrents of bile and sinew as he clenched his stomach and doubled over. He placed his hands over his eyes, and I heard a wet sound from behind them. His eyeballs slid around the sides of his hands, as melted as the rest of his body dissolved in the same way.

It seemed like I should have been afraid, but I wasn't. "That's what you get. No means no."

I sat staring at the simmering pile of flesh he had become until I realized I had to do something with him.

Of course, I called my Uncle Vick. And, of course, he would know what to do.

I heard him drag on his cigarette before he calmly asked, "Where exactly in the swamp are you? Give me some landmarks."

"I can see three double trunk cypresses in a row from here. There's two gators' nests close by, too."

"Alright. I'll be there in about thirty minutes. Stay calm. And sit tight."

The only instruction I didn't follow was the latter. John's body had released its bowels, and the car stank all to be damned. I also hadn't counted on how rank flesh burned from the inside would be.

I never asked Uncle Vick how he got there so fast when I knew we were across town. I suspected he took some kind of shortcut through the swamp, because he arrived on foot.

He looked into the car at what had become of John and repeated my sentiments. "That's good for you, dumbass." Then he unrolled two large tarps he carried under his arms. "Help me get him outta the driver's seat," he instructed, and I did as he said. We took what was left of John and tossed it into the backseat. Uncle Vick spread the other tarp over the soiled driver's seat and slid behind the wheel. "Let's go get this done."

I returned to the passenger seat and rode wordlessly as we wound through an unfamiliar trail through the brush. We were soon at the part of the swamp on Uncle Vick's land. We got out of the car, and he pressed a large stick on the gas pedal. The car rolled out to the middle part of the swamp and began to sink.

I didn't want to cry, but tears streamed down my face.

"Don't worry. Wasn't your fault. He ain't have no business handling you like that. You did what you had to. It's taken care of."

He embraced me in a paternal hug, and I understood this was our secret. I didn't ask about how I had done what I did, but he answered, anyway.

"You're coming into your own. You'll need this."

We never spoke of the incident again, and life went on.

Life going on for me meant I tried dating again. And that's where I fucked up.

Andrea Getz was a real looker. She was the prettiest girl in the school. When she first tried to approach me on the empty walkway to the outside shacks, I wrinkled my nose. She was mean as all get out! Mama had always said pretty is as pretty does, and Andrea's ugliness was marrow deep.

"You just think you something," she sneered.

"I'm a lot. And I ain't everybody's flavor. You biting?" I was certainly physically attracted to her, but she needed to adjust her attitude if we were going to hang out.

Her pretty dark skin turned deep burgundy in her rage. "Oh, you making fun of me? You calling me gay? You got something against me?" She stood half a head taller than me, and before I could clarify or prepare in any way, she launched a right hook that landed right up the side of my head. I went straight down. She kicked me over and over again, punctuating each connection with a new insult.

I kicked out at her legs, and when she went down, I stood up.

Dizzy, I half ran to the main school building to try and get my bearings. She followed me, but didn't attack again because the main halls were monitored.

She proceeded to continue following me through the halls for the rest of that week, yelling insults and threats even as my face swelled and bruised terribly. She never seemed to feel bad about that at all. The biggest insult of it all was that she denigrated me for being queer and wanting her, when I was certain she wanted me, too. Together, we could've ignored everyone else and just done our own thing. Instead, she put me out there and had everybody in my business in a way I didn't like at all.

I felt bad physically, sure, but it really burned that the only other person I had ever been attracted to had turned out to be a piece of shit like the first one. More than that, I hated that I'd let her get the take on me like she had.

"What happened to you?" Uncle Vick asked when I visited the following weekend. Mama had spent the week walking around me and not asking once about what might have happened. I think she was just tired of me always falling into crazy stuff all the time.

"My fucked-up love life went left again."

"Hmmm." He nodded his head slightly. "Hurt you pretty bad, didn't she?"

"Yeah, and not just my feelings. I didn't wanna tell Mama to take me to the doctor, but I do think it's kind of bad. She kicked the shit outta my head."

He moved from his chair and went to one of the many cabinets he kept in the house and withdrew some crushed green stuff. "Take this with a little bit of water. It'll take the swelling down and relieve some pain." He eyed me steadily as I did as he told me. "You think she might try again?"

I shrugged my shoulders, but said, "Yeah, probably. She got it in her head that I hate her being gay. How could that be the case when I was the one trying to chat her up first after watching her follow me around everywhere?" I put my hands on the sides of my head. "I really liked her. But she's a damned psychopath."

"Some people are just bad inside. Can't get out of their own way to be really happy. Invite her here for the weekend. She won't tell anybody she's coming. Then you can have a real conversation with her."

I answered verbally because moving my head still hurt. "Okay."

It all went down just like he said it would. Andrea came the very next day because I sent her a message that we should try to let bygones go by. I tried to send her a follow-up confirmation on directions to the house, but she had already blocked my number. Probably had deleted our text messages, too.

I almost broke when she greeted me, opening the door with that steady gaze of hers that told me how much she really wanted me. Despite my better judgment, I briefly toyed with the idea of forgiving her and trying to get to know her.

She walked around the parlor, touching the furniture and running her hands over the mantle of the fireplace. "This your uncle's place?"

"Yes."

"He home?"

I wasn't quite sure why she asked, but I decided that unless she wanted to make out with me without us being caught, no other reason mattered.

"No. He isn't here." That was true. He had left the house to give us some privacy for whatever was going to go down.

Something flashed in Andrea's eyes, and she walked closer to where I stood, her hands in her jean pockets. "You know, I did like you. Liked, liked you."

I held her gaze. "I figured. I was feeling you, too. Till you tried to kill me."

I hadn't expected her surprised reaction. "You liked me, too? Really?"

No mention of trying to kill me.

"Yeah. You're cute. But you got a fucked-up ass attitude. That ain't cute.

The surprise in her eyes disappeared and was replaced by pure hatred—for me, for herself. For the undeniable attraction that passed between us.

"What you not gonna do is have people talking about me funny. I'm going to the Christian university in Dallas on a full scholarship, and you will keep your mouth shut about any of this."

I shrugged my shoulders, still bewildered by her attitude. "Who would I tell? Doesn't this mean we're both queer, since we're digging on each other? That sounds like a good thing to me."

"It's not." She whipped her hand out of her pocket, brandishing a pocketknife. The handle was well-worn, and I had the feeling she had used it quite a bit. "I'm gonna have to make sure you can't down talk me and ruin my reputation."

She lashed out, and I ducked, rage blinding me. I threw my hand out in front of me. "Stop!"

She froze in action, and sweat began to bead on her nose and forehead as the knife slowly turned back towards her. The tip slid across the front of her throat, easily opening her skin. She continued to dig into the opening, grinding the knife against the bones in her neck. She mouthed something that never emerged audibly because her lips melted into a clump of flesh that oozed towards the floor when she fell.

Soon, Andrea lay spread out gracefully on the cheap throw rug Uncle Vick had spread on the parlor floor that morning. Even with her skin dissolved into mostly unrecognizable features, I could still just make out that broad little nose I had thought was so sexy. The nose ring lay in the middle of the flesh puddle.

Uncle Vick returned, and we wrapped her up in the carpet and took her to the swamp. He sucked on his cigarette and offered me one. I took it.

"There are things we'll have to talk more about. One day."

I took my first puff and inhaled deeply. Instead of burning my windpipe and throwing me into a coughing fit, as I'd always imagined smoking would do, the smoke comforted me, relaxing my nerves.

"Yes."

Graduation came and went, and I never tried to date again. I did try to work every job I could that wasn't fast food or retail. I worked at the laundromat until the day I decided I couldn't look at soap or water ever again, maybe not even to bathe. I tried to deliver mail but got fired when I dumped the mail on the sidewalk to escape from a dog that wasn't leashed. Mama let me take our old mower out around town, but no one wanted to hire a young woman to cut their grass.

I tried a couple of multi-level marketing gigs, first makeup, and then jewelry. The very idea of both of those was outlandish. No one ever needed that much makeup or jewelry in Chriten. At the end of both stints, I ended up with a supply of way too much of both, which I wore in layers around the house while Mama grew sicker of me by the day.

Uncle Vick and I continued our walks around his house and yard. We smoked together in the cemetery and sometimes sat without any words between us for hours. This was our routine, and we loved every minute of it. We passed our time in quiet enjoyment of family, inherited gifts, and solitude.

Then the day came when I walked in on Mama ending a phone call. My usually acerbic mother had tears welling in her eyes.

"Naomi, can you run me to General? Vick done went down bad."

Heart in my throat, I grabbed my keys and ran out the door to start the car before she could say anything else. I had just spent the previous weekend with Uncle Vick, as usual, and he had been just fine.

I hated hospitals, but I hated that my Uncle Vick was in one even more. He was the healthiest person I knew, despite those filtered sticks we both now puffed on. He hated hospitals and knew an herb to help everything. Even Mama broke down and went to the doctor to get her checkups and medicines. It would have taken a terrible event for her brother to agree to go to "the death house," as he called it.

We arrived to see him sitting on the edge of the bed, gently waving the nurses at his side away from him.

"I'm fine. Ain't nothing y'all can do for me here. I'm going home to my own bed." He looked up and saw us in the doorway. "Orlean. Naomi. I'll be ready to go home in a few minutes. They gonna help me get dressed."

There was no use arguing with him. We waited in the waiting room, and as soon as the last nurse left out, he came over. His usually vibrant face had taken on a dull sheen, casting his features into sunken spaces that hadn't been there the last weekend. His steps came slower than I was used to, and panic welled up inside me. He met Mama's eyes, and hers filled with fresh tears. She nodded her head. We all got into my car and went to his house.

I helped Uncle Vick up the steps while Mama opened the front door. We went in, and he dropped heavily into his chair. Mama put her purse on the side table and went into the kitchen.

"How are you feeling, Uncle Vick?" I couldn't stop the words, even though I wasn't sure I wanted to hear the answer. My heart knew something terrible was on the horizon, and my head didn't want to acknowledge it.

He looked at me with the same tenderness and wisdom he always had, his gaze tinged with sadness. "I'm fine. Just fine. I'm home now." He didn't sound fine. I stood beside his chair, my hand in his, until Mama returned to the room with a tray and tea.

"Naomi, can you please go get Vick's bed ready? And get two of the other beds made up for us for the night."

That was my cue to do exactly what she said, without hesitation. They wanted to talk grown folks' business, and I wasn't invited. For the first time I could remember, I didn't want to be privy to their conversation. I didn't want to be grown that night.

I busied myself with straightening up the room. I turned my uncle's bed down and got his slippers from underneath the bed so he wouldn't have to look for them. I took in the ornate, solid wood furniture and vibrant decorations I'd grown up seeing and playing on. The room felt like him and held his scent like a beloved child. So many memories.

I ran my hand along the footboard and then walked over to the armoire. It was my favorite piece in the whole house. It looked like it could be heavier than my small car and worth ten times as much. A sheet of writing paper on the matching desk caught my eye. As usual, I didn't shy away from snooping.

My boldness fled when I read the first words. *Last Will and Testament.*

I almost ran into Mama and Uncle Vick as they slowly entered the room.

"No." I uttered the one word, my heart breaking and my voice failing. "No."

The two of them wrapped me in their arms as I cried. I wanted to be strong like I always was, but I couldn't find the strength to face what was happening.

"Everybody got they time, Naomi," Uncle Vick whispered softly. "Mine is coming."

Mama led us to the bed so we could sit. "Naomi, it'll be okay. This is part of life." I heard the words come from her mouth, but it didn't sound like even she believed what she was saying.

"You can't leave me. You're the only one who understands me. You can get better. Who's gonna walk with me along the swamp and in the graveyard and smoke filters with me? The doctors can fix you…" *Who's gonna continue to fix things for me like he had?*

"Hush, child. Them doctors can't do nothing for me no more. I'm going up yonder soon. And I need you to let me go. I gotta finish getting you ready to take care of this place after I'm gone, and I need to know you'll do that."

I looked at Mama, waiting for an argument from her. I got none.

I sniffed. "I'll do whatever you want me to do."

He nodded. "That's good. I can rest some now. You go on to your bed, and we'll talk more in the morning."

I hugged him again and kissed both him and Mama goodnight.

Before I got out of bed the next morning, I felt in my spirit that Uncle Vick was already gone.

I shambled through the preparations, the ceremony, and the following formalities like a zombie. I felt drained. Mama had stayed at Uncle Vick's house—now, my house—throughout that week, and she was set to leave that last night after the reading of the will. She pressed a thick envelope into my hands. It was just a small part of what Uncle had bequeathed to me.

"Naomi, I know you can be flighty and stubborn, but you have to read this. Tonight. And don't leave this house for nothing, you hear? You gotta understand all this, so everything will be okay."

"Where would I go, Mama? I'm tired. Are you sure you can't stay?"

She shook her head. "No. I can't. You gotta be the one to stay now." The niggling suspicion that Mama knew so much more than she ever let on had finally been confirmed. She spun around and left before I could continue begging.

I locked the door and took the envelope up to Uncle's room, where I'd been sleeping since he'd passed away. I felt closest to him there.

I didn't feel like reading anything right then. The house was too big and too quiet, and I wasn't used to being all alone. I wanted to curl up and sleep until I couldn't sleep anymore. I smoked a couple of our favorite cigarettes. I don't even remember drifting off, but a loud thump woke me some time later.

I sat up in the bed when the sound came again. And again, louder. The envelope fell off my chest and tilted onto the bed. A lone sheet of paper continued to slide out until it lay flat.

Naomi. Read. Now. Aloud.

I picked up the paper and read it.

"I am the bestowed caretaker, and I willingly and humbly submit myself to protecting and preserving my family's gifted inheritance and heritage that lies within and without, until I am unable and pass the honor to another deserving of the same revered blood."

The thumping stopped.

The last shred of sleep slipped away at that realization. I dug around in the envelope and began reading more.

I read the sheets in Uncle Vick's voice.

This will be difficult for me to tell you because I should have told you so much more, so long ago, my dearest niece. I hope you have a cigarette between your fingers now, so you can relax and understand what I'm saying.

When my end came, it was sudden, and it was all I could do to just leave you these instructions. All the other things we shared between us have helped shape you into the position you must now hold.

Ain't nothing free. You'll have enough material wealth to do anything you want, and you must take care of our family for the rest of your life.

Unfortunately, you won't ever be able to marry and move away, or start a family, but I suspect you already know that.

Your powerful gift will only grow stronger as you grow older. Remember that using it will always come at a cost. The price you gotta pay is that of caretaker to our legacy. And this legacy includes an endless list of sins, ones we perpetuated on our own family and others. Those gone before us will only remain at rest as long as we do our duty as caretakers.

It's important that you do just what I say here. Your life, and our entire family's way of life, depend on it.

You can never leave the house and land without first performing the temporary protection spells on the following pages. And even then, you have to make sure to return before they wear off.

If ever the house is left unprotected by the spells or your actual presence, all hell will break loose. I mean exactly what I say here.

You can travel as you want, but you must always come back. You can't spend more than two weeks away, no matter how many layers of protection you cast.
If you ever have guests at the house, you must always stay there with them. If you don't, you are all in danger.

I looked over the following pages with markings I thought I shouldn't know, but that my soul somehow understood.

Danger? Danger from what?

All the words and symbols melted together in my head. I had the barest of ideas what Uncle Vick was talking about, and not for the first time, I hated that family habit we had of beating around bushes and not just getting to the point about things. Even his direct way of speaking had escaped him with that letter.

I grew frustrated. I gripped the sheet of paper in my hand and pulled on my slippers to walk downstairs to take some air on the front porch. The brisk breeze blew around me, and I waited for my head to clear. I focused on movement from the corner of the house.

The scent of rotting flesh assailed me, and I turned my flashlight in the direction the sultry night wind blew from. Years of water damage and swamp creatures had done great damage, but I recognized the hunk of flesh slithering towards me as John, still wearing the remnants of his leather letterman jacket. More shuffling from the graveyard revealed a corpse clad in the deep purple suit with matching shoes and accessories we had just buried Uncle Vick in.

On all sides of him, various corpses dragged themselves from underneath the gravestones bearing the previously unrecognizable names. They moved in ridiculously slow motion, but my brain moved at lightning speed.

Those were his previous lovers.

The other corpses were from our family line.

And I had added two to the dead folks' parade: John, who continued to come toward the porch, and Andrea, who waddled in all her flattened glory from the other end of the swamp.

Realization blanketed me, and I didn't see the two older corpses that approached from the other side, clambering up the porch with bones that rasped against the old wood. The first one embraced me in arms that still had remnants of damp flesh attached, and it opened its mouth as if to chew on me.

I refused to get caught slipping ever again.

I punched the corpse in the face, my fist going through the mangled mouth, past the unhinged jaw, and into the top of the barely clad ribcage. A resisting flow of rancid innards splashed out around my arm, wetting my nightgown. When the second dead person reached my feet, I realized I had to do something else. I couldn't fight my way out of that situation with my fists alone.

I pulled my fist from within the first corpse and kicked it down. Turning the flashlight onto the page I held crumpled in my hand, I read the symbols effortlessly.

As I read, the corpses relaxed and shambled back to where they had been lain to rest. Uncle Vick followed his fellow deceased, and tears filled my eyes. There was a part of me happy to see him one last time, but not like that. I wanted him to rest peacefully.

I wanted all of them to rest. I had to do what I had to do to make sure never to leave the house unprotected again. But I would leave the house. I would travel the world, and I would have grand adventures way outside Chriten, Texas. I'd just do it the right way.

I lit another cigarette and went to the parlor to study my inheritance in detail.

EIGHTEEN
SOMETHING WICKED CAME FOR ME

There are those who will say I'm just too paranoid; that the permeating stench of the "isms"—racism, sexism, ableism, etc.—in my own country made me imagine there was something supernatural happening to me in Romania. I assure you, that isn't the case: something came for me in Romania. Something unspeakable.

I'm used to traversing spaces where I'm the only, or one of a few, Black women in attendance. It has been this way most of my life. I knew there wouldn't be very many Black people in Romania when I planned to travel there for the conference. That knowledge didn't have any bearing on my plans. Different day, same circumstances.

None of that impacted the unique opportunity I had been given to visit Transylvania, a highly desired destination for academics who study horror fiction and the construction of monstrosity. Would I allow a lifetime of misplaced misgivings about my own identity and my relation to the identity of others to stop me from that opportunity?

Of course not. Certainly, I was in more danger on the streets of my own suburban Texan town than I would be thousands of miles away in another country. I had experienced true danger my whole life from folks who deemed me a monster in dark-skinned human form. What purchase could any other real or imagined monsters gain on me?

This doesn't mean I didn't have any misgivings. I had never travelled to Europe, and I wasn't entirely sure what to expect. My flight from Texas carried people of varying races and ethnicities to New York's John F. Kennedy International Airport. The leg to Frankfurt from there involved me and a plane full of more people from other places. Then, I arrived in Frankfurt for my layover, completely aware of my own limitations by being monolingual. No one was unfriendly to me, but no one was overly accommodating, either.

Most everyone around me spoke many languages I could not understand, but they could understand my halting English. I stood out as an outsider, not just because of my skin color, but because of my obvious American-ness and ignorance. Overwhelming relief at hearing a recognized musical hit song from the 80s, piping faintly through the causeway as I stood in front of a display for snacks I didn't recognize, was fleeting but fulfilling. We were all different, and things were as they should be.

Only one other thing would put me at that kind of ease for the rest of my trip.

I looked forward to the six-hour train ride from Bucharest to my final destination in the small town nestled within the Carpathian Mountains. I thought I would catch up on some reading and use the mountainous background to tighten up the presentation I would give in a couple of days. Though the first-class seat was spacious and comfortable, I was unable to focus on the book for more than half an hour.

I grew bored. There were few people sharing the car with me, mostly commuters who came on the train and got off at the next couple of stops. None of them seemed to be on the ride for the longer haul, as I was.

Somewhere between the frequent stops, I dozed lightly. I could not put any dreams into focus, but I awoke with a start, my heart pounding in a way I was unaccustomed to.

Two sets of vibrant, blue eyes stared at me. The two looked so alike, I decided they must be siblings, sharing the same shade of ice blond hair and refined features. They were dressed in fashionable leather, sleek and slender, and wearing the blush of youth.

They looked like any number of my students on campus, with an unfamiliar pallor Texans usually did not maintain in the hot sun. Also, minus the leather, we didn't wear much in Texas. Something about their eyes offset their youthful appearances. Something…wise. Something older than perhaps even the mountain range that ran alongside our train.

I shook my head to divest myself from lingering sleep and foolishness. Of course, they had to be more mature than my students and myself at their age. It was my understanding that Europeans did not stifle their children's wanderlust and encouraged them to have experiences; we did not push our children toward it in the United States. I was sure the two had much more travel and world experience than I. The man smiled at me.

"First class treats us well, yes?" The woman smiled, too, shaming my own smile to my lips. I had been rudely gawking at them, my mouth pursed in what must have been an unpleasant greeting.

They were being very patient for people who were being stared at by a complete stranger.

"Yes, the rhythm of the smooth ride doesn't help much, either." The three of us laughed.

"American?"

I sighed. "Yes. What gave me away, besides my Southern accent and the overabundance of snacks in my bag?"

"We love Americans. The boisterousness, the food, the color." She turned her gaze downward. "I am sorry. I did not mean *your* color…"

"I know. It's fine. I'm happy you two are friendly. I feel a little… out of my element here." The two of them moved into the seats directly across the table from me.

"My name is Andrei, and this is Andreea. We are happy to meet you!" We shook hands across the table. Their grips were strong. Cold. I shivered.

"So, you both are—"

"We are both Andy!" Andreea exclaimed, and we shared another laugh as she read my thoughts.

"My name is Sylvia. Nice to meet you both."

"Is this your first visit to Romania?" Their gaze sharpened and focused on me again. I shifted in my seat, wary of giving too much information to people I had just met, no matter how friendly and beautiful they were.

"Yes. It's beautiful."

"Are you here for holiday?" Andrei flipped his blond hair from his face, and the dim light inside the train caught the angles of his beautiful cheekbones.

"No, for work."

"You must have an amazing job that brings you to our fair country."

I laughed. "Nothing glamorous. I teach humanities at a local college back home."

"Ah! We knew you were an intellectual." They shared an intimate glance between them, and I suddenly realized they were not siblings.

I nodded. "Tell me what you think I need to know most about Romania." Both pairs of eyes lit up, and they spoke at the same time.

"There is so much magic here. Nothing is superficial, and everything holds great meaning and memory."

"You will never visit another place like it in the world."

I listened, rapt, as they told me of their stories and their land. They returned the favor when I described armadillos and barbecue. We posed for a few good-natured selfies to commemorate our meeting. We went on that way for hours, until the train pulled into a tiny station.

"This is our stop. We are happy we met you. Until we meet again." Andrei held my gaze as he and Andreea exited the train. They stood on the platform and waited for the train to pass. I felt their endless blue eyes on me well after they were out of sight.

The sun had long set, and the full moon perched above the train station announced as my destination. There were a few people remaining in the car. One of my fellow passengers, an older woman, frowned in my direction as I struggled to get my suitcase from the rack.

She yelled something at me, repeating herself over and over. Her voice grew louder as she pushed me out the door opposite the one the other passengers exited. I struggled, but she was too strong, and my luggage was too heavy—its momentum from her shove carried me awkwardly down the steps and onto the isolated side of the train.

Before I could figure out what to do or how to alert someone, the train pulled off. I stood alone in the deserted train station. The building across the tracks loomed against the moonlit sky, broken windows observing my abandonment like many eyes. Lights twinkled in the distance, and cool air I had not been prepared for chilled me. I pulled out my phone and clicked on the link for the hotel site. My map soon provided a line of walking directions for me to follow.

I was anxious to warm up. I hoisted one suitcase on top of the other and walked as briskly as I could in the direction the app indicated. After a few minutes, the direction changed. I walked in the new direction, and the map changed yet again. I searched the trees I was supposed to traverse for a path. A stone staircase nestled among the foliage beckoned.

This cannot be any more unnerving than the streets in my town.

The map did not change directions, and I continued my ascent. My back ached from the effort I put into carrying what I then, belatedly, recognized as too much luggage. The trees rustled, and I stopped, checking to see if it was the wind or a creature—creatures—causing the movement. Nothing emerged, and I continued.

I could no longer see the entrance where I started, nor could I see any outlet above me. The stairs wound throughout the trees, the moon providing a faint path where it reflected off the concrete through the tree branches.

"Tante!" The childish voice startled me, and I dropped one of my suitcases. It threatened to totter down the stairs until other children appeared behind me and caught it. Standing on the stairs above me were two older children, perhaps ten or eleven years old. The ones behind me were younger, and it took more of them to gain control of my fallen suitcase.

The older children continued to chant, "Tante," as they relieved me of my baggage. I only retained the tote bag I carried on my shoulder.

No warnings went off in my head. It was late. I was weary. I had been forewarned about pickpockets and should have been more careful on the eerie staircase, among the thick trees, in the dead of night.

But I got no ill feelings from the children. They wanted to help, and they did so cheerfully. I was sure they would want something for doing so, and I was willing to pay them. I just wanted to get to the hotel before daybreak.

The children hummed as we made our way up the stairs in a luggage-laden train, much like the one I had ridden in on earlier. I don't know how long it took us, as it seemed forever, but realistically, it would have only been minutes.

We finally emerged on a cobblestone street, underneath dim streetlights that illuminated my little helpers. The older ones graciously took the bills I offered. They left, disappearing around the corner of one of the larger buildings.

"What may I have?" The smallest of the children lamented. I turned to face him, and his wide eyes reflected black and large underneath the street light.

"I've already given your friends some money."

"Yes, but they will not share it with me." I felt pity for him, but I had no more cash to spare. He eyed the bag of snacks sticking up from my tote.

"Would you like a snack?" His face lit up, and he nodded. I pulled the bag from my shoulder and held it open so he could see what I had inside. He rummaged around for a few seconds and then pulled out a meat snack.

He grasped his treasure and smiled at me, small teeth glinting in the night air. Small, sharp teeth, stunning in their shape. I inhaled raggedly. He turned and ran away.

I stood on the cobblestone to catch my bearings, checking the map on my phone again. The arrow now pointed downward; down the sloping street, I was almost sure, ran parallel to the stairs we had arduously climbed. I followed it, dragging my bags behind me, taking comfort in the way the wheels tumbled over the stones and how the echo followed me to the hotel so I would not be alone again.

I verified the address on the map and released one of my bags to use the knocker outside the heavy wooden double doors. It was not long before a burly man opened the door and greeted me with a smile. He grabbed my bags, and for the second time that night, I allowed a stranger to help me, entrusting him to be as good-natured as the children had been.

A cheerful woman stood behind the counter. "Hello! We are happy you finally made it in. Mrs. Lebbon, yes? We were worried you caught a later train."

I nodded and paused to gather my thoughts. "I came in on the midnight train, as scheduled. It just took me a while to get here."

The woman frowned and took a second glance at her watch.

The man went behind the counter and brought out a tray with shot glasses and a slender glass bottle. "Drink? To your safe arrival?"

"Yes, please." He poured the three of us an offering and nodded. "Palinka. The best we have available."

Still trying to warm up, I downed the liquid and relished the way the sharp alcohol started to warm me from the inside out.

"Thank you for your kindness. I had a delightful conversation with two fellow travelers on the train. But then I was thrown off the train at the station on the wrong side. Then, my map took me on an adventure, up some stairs, through the forest with children, and onto the street above. There was likely an easier way to get here, but I came the hard way."

The woman narrowed her eyes. "You met people on the train?"

"Yes. A young couple. Andreea and Andrei. They entertained me until they got off."

The man and woman exchanged a glance. Her hands began to tremble.

"When you got off the train, you were pushed?"

I waved my hand. "An older lady may have been irritated because I was moving so slowly. She pushed me off the train on the opposite side from the station."

My chill returned when the both of them gasped in unison.

"What of these children? Where did they come from?" The ruddy color had run from the man's face, and he looked almost as pale as my young friends from the train.

"I don't know where they came from, but they met me on the stone stairs and helped me with my luggage coming up. They were sweet. I was thankful for the help."

The woman crossed herself. She and the man both made spitting gestures, three times, to their side. I did not see any liquid. She placed a heavy skeleton key on the counter between us.

"My husband and I will take you to our largest room. It has a nice fan for if you get hot. Under no circumstances are you to open the windows to your room while you are here. Not at night, and not in the day." Her voice was grave as she spoke, precisely and slowly so I could understand her words.

I had no interest in opening any windows. I only wanted to shower and go to bed. I nodded.

She gripped my wrist, and her eyes bore into mine. "I need to know you understand what I am telling you. You must only open your door in the daytime. Keep everything closed at night."

"Yes. I understand." The palinka was starting to relax my already exhausted body. I followed the pair to a well-appointed room in the main part of the hotel. They opened the door for me and pulled my luggage inside.

"Remember, do not open your door for any reason at night. Especially not tonight."

"Why especially not tonight?" It was an odd clarification, one that seeped through my exhaustion.

The two shared a look before the woman responded. "It is just not safe for a woman travelling alone, yes?"

Extra caution made sense in that respect. "Yes. Thank you."

As soon as they left, I had no more energy to entertain showering. It was no wonder I was exhausted—it was four in the morning! My adventures had taken four whole hours. I stripped off my outer clothing and sank into the soft coverings of the bed, succumbing to sleep.

My exhaustion and the delicious palinka did not guarantee me a sound rest. I tossed and turned, struggling against something beckoning me from—where, I did not know. I unwrapped myself from the bedding and went to use the restroom.

The wind whistled outside the hotel, humming. And calling my name.

Sylvia.

That couldn't be right. No one in that foreign country knew my name except the hotel owners. But they wouldn't be calling for me. They had made sure I promised them I wouldn't open my door or windows.

Just outside the windows, I heard tapping. Gentle at first, then more insistent.

The room that had previously been a comfortable temperature prodded me with iciness. I slowly walked to the window, careful to only touch the curtain and not the window.

A flurry of movement on the other side of the cloth caught me unaware, and I stumbled backward.

Sylvia.

The still bright light of the moon caught shadows outside the window, casting the shapes on the curtain. Humanoid figures swirled, a pair in unison. Beautiful. Wispy. Calling.

I went back to the window and watched the shadows as several others joined the dancing pair. Smaller, more urgently moving, child-like—followed by a large female shape that closely resembled the old woman who had pushed me from the train.

My breath came in shallow spurts as I watched the forms clash and dissipate, to reassemble on the curtains of the other windows along the wall.

Sylvia.

More insistent. I walked backward to the bed and grabbed my phone. *Who would I call?*

I opened the lock screen and went to my camera, thinking to catch the events on film. The thumbnail of the last picture I had taken, back on the train, smiled at me. I enlarged it. I was in the picture alone, smiling. I looked at the others, looking for the Andys. They weren't in any of the pictures.

The syllables of my name became something elongated outside the window, forming sounds no longer recognizable except as those of a battle. There was a fight going on under the full moon. And I would gratefully miss it. Nothing could move me back to the window to see anything else.

I understood all I needed to in those last hours of night before sunrise. In my naiveté, I had placed myself in danger, inviting the damned to join me in conversation. The old woman and the children —could they be called a woman and children?—saved me from a fate of eternal damnation. Something wicked came for me in the ancient mountains of Romania, and others, not quite so wicked as they, saw fit to help a traveler in her ignorance.

NINETEEN

SAD, SPOOKY SALLY

CW: CHILD ABUSE/CSA

"Mommy, Savvy went potty two times in her dipey."

Three-year-old Tariq Smith made the admission in a tiny voice just above a whisper, hoping that his Mommy heard him and would help. His baby sister was only a year old, and she whined a lot due to the broken rash that perpetually remained in her diaper area.

"Shut up all that damned noise!" Their mother bellowed from the other end of the apartment.

"But we hungry, too, Mommy." He clung to the door jamb with sticky, cold hands. Tears rolled down his chubby cheeks. Savanah's whimper revved up into a full-blown cry. Tariq held her hand and looked around the room for a fresh diaper. Savanah was more than half his size, but he thought he might be able to figure out how to put her diaper on if he found one. He regularly changed his own diapers.

"Can't you make them be quiet?"

Tariq didn't recognize the man's voice and couldn't tell if he was a nice man or not. He sounded mean, and most of the visitors their mother had over were mean to them. Tariq had to assume that man would be mean to them, too. Mommy usually didn't let the men hit them, but whenever one of the men hit Mommy first, he always came to find Tariq and Savanah.

The pain searing the tender flesh of Sally's abdomen sliced sharper than the scythe she had just swung to cut the brush at her feet. She doubled over and tried to stop the overwhelming waves of nausea rushing over her. She had ignored the ever-increasing intensity of the cramps and kept her pace with the others around her, thinking that if she pretended the baby was not coming, then it simply would not be.

Tati Jane, the plantation's healing woman, had told her what to expect. She could only remember certain parts because, at ten years old, she had no point of reference for much of the information. Also, having the knowledge—whether remembered or not—and going through the actual experience were different things.

She almost wished to feel the bite of the whip between her shoulder blades to take her focus from what was happening within her body. Sally was young, but her stubbornness had already resulted in two lengthy sessions at the whipping post. The first time, she was punished because she had taken an extra biscuit from the house dinner table.

Tati Jane always ate so little, and Sally thought a little bit of extra food might help the elderly woman get over the malaise she had currently been suffering. She never had the chance to see if it would have helped because David, the master's eldest son, had told on her and slapped the biscuit from her hands before smashing it into the hardwood of their kitchen floor.

He then spat on the ruined bread and punched her in her temple before grabbing her by her hair and dragging her into the sitting room, where his father sat, waiting to hear about her transgression. Master ordered David to take her out and whip her, himself, so he could start asserting his dominance around the plantation. It had not mattered to them that she was but a child, so young her budding breasts had not yet bloomed.

It also had not mattered that she was too young to have even had her second monthly flux: she was not too young for David, and then Isiah, the master's younger son, to take turns hurting her down under her clothes after David whipped her. She had fought both men to try to keep them from violating her, to no avail. The both of them took her back out to the post and whipped her until she passed out. She awakened to a burning sensation across her back as it was pressed over and over again into the hard dirt, and more pain between her legs as David pulled his trousers on and Isaiah rose and fell on top of her. She was in far too much pain to fight them off the second time.

As a result, she was having a baby. Sally never cried out while they were hurting her, and she did not cry out as the contractions grew stronger. She continued to swing the scythe well after the rush of warmth ran down her legs, and the greedy soil beneath her feet consumed her life-bearing fluids. Harsh grunts escaped her throat even as she tried to hold them back. The woman nearest her almost missed catching Sally as her body failed, and she swooned, clutching her tightened belly as she fell to the moist ground.

Cecilia Smith stomped into the room. "I done told y'all to go to bed and quit all that noise! I'm gonna call that ghost lady to come get y'all."

Mommy was angry. She was always angry.

"Don't call the ghost lady, Mommy. I tried to change Savvy's dipey but I made a mess. I'm sorry, Mommy." Tariq stood over his baby sister, where she lay playing with her dirty diaper on the floor, grasping the contents clumsily in her hands and moving towards her mouth. Tariq brushed at her hands until she dropped the refuse back onto the floor. He didn't want to leave his spot over her in case

Mommy decided to spank him. She often hit both of them so they would cry and fall asleep.

Cecilia grabbed his chubby arm and pinched him so hard he cried out. "I'm calling old spooky Sally now. Sally! Come get these bad ass kids!"

Sally pushed the way Tati Jane told her to, gripping the sweaty bedclothes in her aching fists. Nothing had ever hurt the way trying to birth the baby did. She tried to focus on doing what she was told, but she wanted instead to escape from her tortured body and leave the husk to wither in the pain that threatened to destroy it.

Finally, something inside her burst free, and the baby fell out and into Jane's competent hands, waiting at Sally's feet. The older woman rubbed the baby with an old cloth, and his indignant screams echoed through the dank cabin. The pain became a distant memory, and another feeling replaced it inside Sally. She raised up slightly to see what the baby looked like. Now that he was no longer housed inside her body, she started to think of him as a separate being from her, one she longed to get to know.

"Boy. Big, strong, strapping boy." Jane wrapped the baby in another cloth and pressed him into the space Sally's arm made as she half reclined on the cot. Jane eased her down, back into her delivery position, so she could finish her work. As she pressed on Sally's still swollen abdomen, the girl watched the baby in awe. She took in his tiny face and head, still shaped like a cone where he had passed from her body. She weakly unwrapped the cloth to examine his hands. She wanted to see his feet and his legs, but she was afraid to completely unwrap him.

Sally loved the baby, despite the circumstances that had brought him to her. She went back out to the field after two days of bed rest, afforded the additional time only because Jane had to stitch her up after the birth. It hurt for her to walk, but David had come into the cabin yelling that she had to get back to her duties. Jane showed her how to make a sling for the baby so she could carry him outside with her and allow him to feed while she worked.

The miracle of birth had given her ample milk to feed her son, and he grew fat in the first month. She talked to him and told him the stories she had heard around the plantation, tales of freedom and royal ancestors. Sally was a quick learner and took to caring for the baby easily. She still marveled at his perfection and often spent long hours in the night looking at him, dreaming of his freedom one day as she drifted off to sleep.

On one such night, the master came into the cabin she shared with other slave women and told the others to get out. Sally tried to free herself from the bondage of slumber to comprehend what was happening. The man wrenched her baby from her arms and handed him off to David, who had followed him inside.

"Time to get that one off to the Pendersons." The baby started to wail, and Sally's breasts tingled in response, milk blooming on the front of her dress. Master eyed the growing spots and fumbled with his belt. He pushed Sally back down onto her cot and raped her as she cried out for her baby. The sticky milk running from her breasts covered the front of his shirt. She could not stop him from defiling her.

Sally closed her eyes and found she could almost allow herself to escape her body to go and try to find her son, to see where they were taking him. She had never heard of the Pendersons, and she did not know the whereabouts of their plantation. She did not know where to look. Knowing she would likely never see him again hurt her soul much more than Master had hurt her body.

"Mommy! No. I'm sorry. I'm sorry. Her dipey was hurting her."

Cecilia glanced at Savanah and bent to take a look at the baby's bottom through the unsecured side of her diaper. Tariq hadn't been able to close it. She sucked her teeth and went to the rickety chest of drawers in front of the lone window in the room and rummaged around the top. The tube of diaper ointment she grasped was flattened, but she squeezed it, anyway, putting the tiny drop of cream on her daughter's buttocks and fastening the diaper.

"We hungry." Tariq sniffled and held his arm where she had pinched him. He backed away from Cecilia when she turned her gaze to him. Her face had softened slightly, and she returned to the chest of drawers. She brushed small roaches off the open packet of crackers and handed them to Tariq.

"Share with your sister. Y'all eat these and go to sleep." Cecilia located two bottles with murky liquid inside. She sprinkled a sample onto her hand and tasted it. "And take these."

Tariq had already tried to get Savanah to drink the warm, leftover lemonade in her bottle, but she had thrown it across the room and whined. He agreed with her that it was nasty. But he didn't tell Mommy that. He sat down and broke a hard cracker into two pieces, and handed one to his little sister.

Satisfied, Cecilia closed the door. This time, she locked it behind her.

Sally had just turned eleven when she had the twins. Two beautiful baby girls with heads full of kinky curly hair. Tati Jane sucked her teeth as she worked to stop Sally's bleeding that time, muttering under her breath about devils and hellfire. The birth had been difficult on Sally's young body, but she felt all the struggle had been worth it when she held her daughters. She envisioned them growing up healthy, released from the bondage of slavery. Sally heard the slaves talking in their quarters, and several openly discussed a day when they would be freed people. Freedom. To grow. To love. To see her babies grow up this time, into women who would go on to raise families of their own.

She sang to her daughters as they nestled deeply inside a special sling Tati Jane crafted just for Sally. She returned to the field after a week, due to the extensive damage her body sustained carrying and delivering two babies at her young age. Sally could not move as quickly as she had before their birth. She tried to keep up and stay out of the memory of Master and Isiah and David. She did her work and kept her head down, not even engaging in conversation with her fellow enslaved people. She only wanted to sing to her babies and feed them, willing herself to live more fully in the imagined world she desired for their future.

Sally and her daughters did not remain invisible for long. David came to her in the field one day when the babies were a few weeks old and snatched them from their mother's breasts. Sally howled and beat helplessly at him as he headed toward the big house carrying her most precious cargo. Isiah intercepted them and pulled out the whip he loved to carry. His vicious lashes burned across her face, her still leaking breasts, her abdomen. He struck her over and over again until she lay prone in the yard, a bloodied, heartbroken mass.

She never saw her daughters again.

The master and David and Isaiah continued to violate Sally relentlessly, and she remained pregnant every year until she was twenty. Each time her births produced live babies, the men took them away from her. Sally spent more and more time outside her body than inside, where the pain of her childlessness seared her soul. After the last birth, Tati Jane pronounced Sally's womb exhausted, and she could not bear any more children.

David decided she would then go to work in the big house since his wife had just had their son, and Sally could help feed him and take care of their toddler while his wife convalesced. He also figured it would be easier to get to Sally when he wanted her to perform other duties if she were already inside the house and not out in the cabins.

Wordlessly, Sally acquiesced and followed him to her new charges. She listlessly picked the infant up in her arms and held her to her breast when the baby cried. Her milk production, meant solely for her own babies, did not respond to the baby, and soon there were only trickles coming down. She spent long days chasing the toddler with the infant hanging from her breast because their mother did not want to spend any time with them.

Then came the night Sally escaped her mortal coil. She was no longer tethered to her tortured life of bondage. She knew true freedom for the first time in her life. When Sally awakened the next morning, she felt excitement for the first time in years. She had not felt anything since her last baby was stolen—they took the last of her life from her with him. Now she was renewed, ready for a new life. With all her babies.

Kneeling in front of the cot where the toddler slept, she held a feather pillow over his head until his small body stopped fighting. She picked the infant up and held her tightly against her bosom, covering her little face until she, too, became still. She pressed kisses onto their sweet little faces and then walked down the stairs and into the yard underneath the hanging tree.

"What have you done, you Black bitch?"

David's hoarse cries woke the entire plantation. Isaiah followed quickly behind him with his trusty whip. Sally could hear David's wife wailing from inside the house, but she sounded far away. David kicked her until she fell down. Sally hummed, and Isaiah cracked his whip on the other side of her body.

"Get a rope!" Isaiah yelled to one of the enslaved house boys, and the child ran to do as he was told.

Master joined the melee and barked additional orders. "You are going straight to hell! I damn you for all eternity!"

Sally forced a laugh from between her swollen lips. "I have been in hell. Now I will be redeemed. I will find my babies, and we will be free."

The three men wrapped the retrieved rope around her neck and dragged her to the big tree in the yard. David continued to pummel her with blows until his father moved him so they could complete Sally's punishment.

She had left her body long before Master pronounced her death.

David, Isaiah, and the enslaved people gathered in the yard locked their astonished gazes on a figure retreating from where they stood. Sally walked away from them, holding David's daughter in one arm and holding the hand of a small boy with her free hand. David's son and two other children walked solemnly behind Sally's apparition, as her body hung from the tree, swaying in time to her mournful lullaby carried by the wind, drifting away with her and her children.

Tariq heard a sweet song coming from somewhere outside the bedroom window. He went to see where it was coming from. Mommy always told them to stay out of the windows, but he had to see. It wasn't Mommy. She never sang to them. A nice lady was calling him and Savanah. He stood on his tiptoes, and he could see her clearly, where she stood under the streetlight, waving to him.

"My babies. Come with me so we can be together forever."

She was so pretty. For the first time in a week, Tariq wasn't hungry anymore. And he was warm. He gently shook Savanah awake and took her to the window with him. His baby sister cooed and babbled to the pretty lady. She had other kids with her, and they all rose high in the night sky until they were right outside the eighth-floor window, smiling at Tariq and Savanah.

"My beautiful babies. Come." She stretched out her hand, and Tariq helped Savanah up onto the window ledge and into the woman's arms. He followed, warmed by her embrace. Happy to be with other children. She would take care of them.

"Now, we must go get my other babies."

Cecilia Smith stepped into the room just in time to watch her two children disappear into the arms of the woman floating in the window.

TWENTY
HIGHER EDUCATION

SPRING SEMESTER, WEEK 1

I hope this class can fly under administrative radars and stay small. Eight students for a composition class is a perfect size, regardless of what the powers that be thought. I smirked as I thought of how we community college writing professors were expected to do unlimited institutional service, teach five classes every semester, each with twenty-five students, assign four major essays, and teach writing as a process that included invention, drafting, and revision.

That couldn't realistically happen with high-class caps. Eight students meant I could do all those things and more for my students. I did my job for the students and always wanted what was best for them and their learning. It was a challenge to show them I really had their best interests in mind when I was overwhelmed with grading and institutional service.

"Hello, new colleagues. Welcome to our course. I won't bore you by reading our syllabus to you. You can read it on your own sometime before we meet again. Instead, I want to get started learning more about each other. Let's do some writing."

To my surprise, there were no blank faces staring at me after my introductory spiel. No grumbles over the first ice-breaker exercise, either. Hooray! These both boded well for a positive experience in the class for me and the students. This semester just might be my best, ever.

SPRING SEMESTER, WEEK 3

"Good morning, colleagues! How is everyone doing today?"

"Good."

"Okay."

"Fine."

"Tired."

Thumbs up.

"Excellent! I'm glad the energy in here is so positive this morning. I'll need to borrow some of that while I try not to get frustrated over my car being hit from behind last evening. The driver had the nerve enough to drive away without seeing if I was okay." I would have shaken my head in my customary manner, but my neck was still sore from the impact. Instead, I wagged my finger at the offender, as if they could see me from wherever they had run to.

"Oh, no!"

"Are you okay, Professor?"

I placed my hand over my heart and performed a slight bow of gratitude without bending my neck. "I'm okay. Thank you for asking. My car's back bumper isn't. And my old joints aren't too happy about the whiplash, but slow driving, heating pads, and rest are helping a lot."

I looked over the classroom to take attendance. New faces stared at me expectantly.

"Ah! I'm sorry for the gloom and doom this morning. Welcome to our newcomers! If you would, please, hang around for a few minutes after class so I can get you caught up to where we are on assignments. I promise we aren't always talking about such dramatic things in our course."

So much for flying under the radar with a manageable class size.

Two new students. I guess the dean's admins didn't bother to email me to ask if it was okay to place the students since my class was so far from the maximum. I tried not to grow perturbed at having been disregarded in that way. Things changed so often on our campus that I wasn't even sure if it was still a regulation that they had to notify me and gain my approval beforehand once the semester had already started.

"Are there any questions on our last discussion? Anyone besides our newest members?"

Low murmuring started. I knew there would be questions. Questions were good for emerging writers to ask: it was a sign they were doing the reading and working through the concepts we discussed.

Knowing how reticent students usually were to speak up in class about anything, I stayed ready to answer as many questions as they could possibly come up with.

"I'll pass around the roll sheet while you think a little bit."

I gave them a few moments to compose themselves. There was little fidgeting, some murmuring, but mostly, questioning glances as they looked around to determine who would go first.

"Now, what questions do you have for me?"

SPRING SEMESTER, WEEK 5

"Many apologies, my esteemed colleagues. I will not be able to attend class this week due to a minor injury I've sustained. I'm okay, but I have to rest for a few days. Please keep track of our discussions and assignments online, and if you need me, please feel free to text or email me. See you next week!"

I lowered my dimmed laptop screen and removed my glasses. The headache stemming from the knot on the back of my head throbbed in response to the effort I'd had to use to type the announcement in our learning management system.

I didn't make it a habit to miss class often, and I hated to do so then. If I could have navigated my way to work without having to drive myself, I would have gone in, concussion or not.

The crash of my head against the corner of my home office desk the previous night had rattled me in more ways than one. I lived alone, with two cats, neither of which could really help me if I had a medical emergency. They both were off playing elsewhere in the house when I blanked out and fell from my chair. I hadn't realized I had fallen until I was pushing myself up off the floor, head pounding, vision blurred.

I was relatively healthy, but middle age had come and waned in the face of the winter of my years. Other professors my age usually retire to do important things. The most important task I had was to get my students ready to tackle the world they lived in through their writing. I wanted to be around to continue doing that for a long time.

SPRING SEMESTER, WEEK 7

"Are you okay, Professor? Like, really okay?"

"We're worried about you."

"Yeah! First, that car accident, and then another injury."

Their concern touched me deeply, and I was appreciative of working with such compassionate young adults. I heard enough about how this generation was so entitled and selfish from my co-workers. They didn't know the students like I did. They couldn't appreciate that these young adults were no more selfish than any of us were at their age. They were actually more empathetic than I remember my own generation being.

"It does seem I've had a pretty rough few weeks, doesn't it?"

I dimmed the front room lights and took off my sunshades, replacing them with my regular glasses.

"I really appreciate you all. I'm recovering now, but I have the best job in the world, working with the best people." I pointed at them and offered a slight bow that didn't set my new headache off to higher heights. "As long as we keep these lights down and speak quietly, I'll be okay. Now, let's do some writing."

The newest set of students who never said anything in class didn't join in the quiet applause.

SPRING SEMESTER, WEEK 9

Time to take a long walk across campus to the dean's suite after class today. An email wouldn't suffice for what I had to say. Four more new students had been placed in my class beyond the halfway mark of the semester. There was no way to get them to the same point to where the rest of the class was. Their names didn't even appear on my official roll for the course. This placement was a serious injustice to them, and I was dedicated to their success. I'd gladly fight this fight for them.

"Fernando, did you have any thoughts on this reading?"

The newer students were still quiet in class. I didn't typically cold call on students like that, but if I didn't call on these, they'd never raise their hands.

Another hand shot up.

"Okay, Fernando. Not feeling it today?" I pointed at the hand in the air. "Yes?"

"Professor, who's Fernando?"

I wrinkled my brows and paused. "Our colleague. You aren't Fernando."

"You called someone else Fernando during the last class period, too."

"I did?"

Several students nodded.

I sighed. "I'm sorry. You all know I'm still recovering from that head injury. Thank you for your grace with an old woman."

I pointed to Lucas again. "You wanna help us out on this reading, Lucas?"

SPRING SEMESTER, WEEK 11

The incessant headaches and blurred vision with regular bouts of dizziness after my fall made it difficult to do much more than come in to work each class day and go back home, straight to bed. I'd fallen severely behind on grading assignments, and my anxiety stayed high, worrying about catching up. My administration had been understanding of my current health situation so far, but I didn't want to push their benevolence. All I wanted was to feel better again, to help my students as best I could.

Two more new faces greeted me when I peeked into our open classroom door. I stepped into the classroom. They waved, chattering among one another. That was new, but I was glad they'd finally opened up some.

My happiness over their social progress tanked when I realized I'd walked in on my dean speaking from the podium.

"...our counselors are here on campus if any of you need to work with them. I'm so sorry for our loss."

I was busted.

I opened my mouth to ask her if we could talk in the hall, where I could explain myself, plead my case for being so far behind on grading assignments and returning feedback to the students. I thought I'd have a chance to at least meet with her about the situation before she let me go.

She gestured towards the door I'd just entered through.

"Professor Larson will finish out the semester with you. Please join me in welcoming him."

He stood at my podium. "I just want to introduce myself and give you my contact information. I'm working on getting your grades caught up in the system. We will take the rest of the week off to visit the counselors or process everything. Professor Thomas was a beacon of light for us all."

I had never seen Professor Larson on campus.

Fernando raised his hand for the first time that semester.

"Yes, Fernando?" I whispered. I couldn't remember how I knew his name, or the names of the other students looking at me expectantly. Their names had never shown up in the learning management system or our official class roster. I just *knew* their names.

"We're ready to start class now, Professor."

The group of newer students nodded in affirmation, and their light chatter drowned out that of the other students and their new professor.

I cleared my throat. For the first time in weeks, my head was no longer pounding. My stiff neck relaxed, and my shoulders dropped. The excitement of sharing and learning and renewed energy coursed through me. I adjusted my glasses.

The students always came first, and I was happy to still be able to fight this fight with them. For them.

"Okay. Let's do some writing."

TWENTY-ONE

WELCOME

The unseasonably high winds blew the corner of the mat, so the letters in the beginning were covered. Rheeta stood back from her front door to survey her newly inspired décor. She hadn't decorated the yard since the kids were in middle school, and now that the last of them was gone away from home, having something to focus on other than the loneliness of her empty nest spurred her excitement about mundane things like mats and garden accessories.

She bent down to straighten the "Welcome" mat so that it read more than "come." Rheeta had always teased the kids that she never put out a mat before, so that their friends couldn't read and interpret it to mean they were supposed to come to their house every day. "Until I can find a 'please bring food—starving teens' mat, I'll keep using the generic ones without any messages."

Her babies, birthed and found, had known she was joking because all the friends had always ended up in Rheeta's gameroom to hang out, anyway. Eating her out of house and home. Sometimes breaking things that had to be replaced. Definitely harassing poor old Harry, their long-suffering dog. In the end, it was all in good fun. She missed the chaos of a house full of rambunctious teens running around with a small elephant masquerading as a dog.

Her Louis had often been right in the middle of the disarray, introducing the next generation to the virtues of old school hip hop music and jigsaw puzzles. He lit up when he was able to provide anything for the kids and their friends. And for Rheeta. That husband of hers had held an impeccable work ethic that had driven her nuts sometimes, but mostly kept her worried for him.

That worry came to pass when he suffered a heart attack in the warehouse he supervised and died instantly. Rheeta always thanked goodness he hadn't suffered or lingered. He would have hated wasting away, with her having to care for him in a sickbed. The way he went was the way he would have wanted. And her last memory of him before the closed casket ceremony was of virility, him unfolding his large frame from their bed that morning, kissing her on the forehead.

Her smile faltered a bit. A part of her hoped that maybe someone *would* see the sign on her doorstep and come visit with her for a little while.

The kids had scattered in the four years since Louis had passed, and Rheeta wouldn't have had it any other way. She'd often joked with her husband that they were supposed to raise their kids to leave them, to live independent lives. Louis would jump up and down in a faux victory dance and exclaim, "Well, hot dog! We're on our way to a retirement filled with lazy days and good food nobody else will eat before we can get to it."

She'd swat at him playfully. "As if you're ever going to retire."

He'd kiss her and exclaim, "Of course I will. Then we can spend forever together, doing nothing except whatever we want."

Their forever never came, and now Rheeta faced her autumn and winter years all alone. She folded her arms across her torso against the chill in the air that blew the leaves in the yard up into a swirl. The mat folded over again. *Come.*

The wind blew her front door wide open, and it banged on the wall, startling her. She stepped over the mat, half-heartedly trying to move it back into place before giving up in the onslaught of the kick in the air. She closed the door and locked it, standing in the foyer of her family home.

Memories washed over her. Of her and Louis touring the inventory home when she was pregnant with their daughter, their third child, wondering if they would ever grow into the enormous space of five bedrooms and three and a half baths. Of bringing the baby home. Finding out she was already pregnant with the last child at the baby's first birthday party that they held in the yard. It was baby number last who covered the foyer wall with little brown paint handprints. The massive formal dining room table sat solitary in the room that used to be alive with fancy family meals that Rheeta insisted on cooking regularly so they could eat together. The slight sprinkling of dust reminded her to clean soon.

The scent of Louis' cologne assaulted her nose, and she swooned against the stained glass center of the door. She had first bought it for him when they visited Cabo, years ago, and she smelled it as they walked through the airport on the way to the resort.

"You spoil me, sweet wife of mine." His white teeth beamed from between those sensuous, thick lips that Rheeta loved.

"It's selfish, really. Now I have an excuse to get close to you all the time so I can smell you."

"You never need an excuse."

The scent enveloped her. She could feel his presence around her, and her heart fluttered. What she wouldn't give to be held by him once again.

The familiarity faded, and she was once again in her lonely reality in a giant, empty house. Needing solace, she decided it was the perfect evening for a cup of tea before bed.

She turned the porch light on. Humming to lift her spirits, she went to the large kitchen she'd always loved and put the teakettle on the stove, laughing as she put a mug on the counter next to it.

Her oldest daughter had bought her one of those fancy coffee makers that heated water and poured it through little plastic pods. "Ma, it's faster, and the tea tastes just as good."

It might be faster, but the tea did not taste as good. She used the machine whenever one of the kids decided to visit, which wasn't very often. Otherwise, it sat alone on the counter as she continued to use her old, stainless steel teapot on the stove.

Rheeta wiped down the space around the sink and washed the lone glass nestled inside. She then busied herself with putting it and the scant few dishes in the rack up into the cabinets.

Something large brushed against her legs, and she grasped the counter to regain her balance. Harry used to love running between her and the counters in the kitchen, as if he were a small dog that could easily fit into small spaces.

He wasn't small at all, weighing in at around 100 pounds. She felt the familiar sensation again, and tears welled up in her eyes. She missed Harry almost as much as she missed Louis. Her husband had gifted him to her one Christmas, and her special boy had mourned the loss of their Louis together. Harry was already elderly, but she knew he had held on to help her as much as he could.

Finding him dead at the foot of her bed had almost destroyed her. He had gone peacefully, wrapped up in one of Louis's favorite blankets. It was a befitting end to a valiant companion who had put up with their kids because he loved her and Louis. She was sure he had loved the kids, too, but he was her boy. She lifted her eyes towards the mantle on the fireplace where both his and Louis's urns sat, in spots of honor, where she could keep them around.

A slight sound to her side in the kitchen caught her attention. She turned around and gasped. The mug she'd placed beside the stove was filled with steaming water.

Rheeta hadn't filled the cup. The teapot hadn't even gone off. The water she could see through the glass top as she walked closer popped sporadically with the faintest beginnings of a boil that hadn't yet flourished.

She didn't want tea anymore.

She turned the fire off. Unable to bring herself to touch the mug to dump and wash it, she left it sitting where it was.

She turned and walked slowly into the living room to watch television. She sat down in the recliner she had inherited upon Louis' death and sighed. She debated raising her feet, thinking of her grandmother, who always insisted that her feet stay on the floor. "Feet wasn't meant to be propped up like that. Makes a body lazy." Granny's voice whispered in her ear, and Rheeta sat straight up.

The wide screen of the television came on, stunning Rheeta. Her eyes searched frantically for the remote control so she could turn it off. Before she could find it, the television screen went blank again.

Rheeta could hear a faint hum, picking up the tune she was humming to herself in the kitchen. The tone was ominous. That wasn't her Louis. Or Granny. Definitely not Harry. Not waiting around to hear it get louder or become identifiable, she walked as quickly as she dared to her bedroom and slammed the door shut. One of the hardest things about growing older was not being able to make your body do the things you wanted it to do, and as badly as she wanted to break into a run, she knew it to be unsafe while she was at home alone. Always alone.

She waited long moments with her back against the bedroom door, rationalizing what had happened.

The television was old. Maybe it had a short. She probably just forgot she had already poured the water into her mug. The water in the kettle was hotter than she thought. She was thinking of her dead beloveds, and they had come to comfort her. They hadn't meant to scare her. They loved her. And wanted her to know they were still with her.

A loud crash and the sound of breaking ceramic came from the kitchen, and Rheeta eased away from the door, deeper into her bedroom. Another door slammed somewhere else in the house. Something rustled in the hallway outside her bedroom door. Multiple sets of footsteps ran up, closer. Closer. They stopped right outside the door.

Silence.

Rheeta trembled and waited for the noise to start up again. She thought of calling one of the kids to come over, but embarrassment stopped her. They would tell her she was imagining things. And start up about her selling the house, again. In that moment, she knew they were probably right. The house was too much for her alone. She didn't need all the space. She'd contact a realtor first thing in the morning.

She didn't call anyone right then. She stood in her bedroom with her hands pressed over her mouth, willing herself to breathe while the destruction of her house continued behind the door.

After the longest time, she realized whatever was happening might be over. Rheeta went into her bathroom and brushed her teeth with shaky hands. She always showered in the evenings or took a long bath. She didn't do either and instead pulled on her nightgown and burrowed underneath her covers. Sleep came more easily than it usually did, and Rheeta didn't have time to wonder how she could sleep in the middle of the madness overtaking her. She welcomed the slumber.

Three loud knocks pounded on her bedroom door. Rheeta couldn't shake the cover of sleep and mumbled.

"Come in."

The kids always waited until she was deep into sleep to come asking for stuff in the middle of the night.

The door to her bedroom slammed open. Rheeta sat up, fully awake.

The kids weren't at home anymore. She was alone.

Flurries of whispers met her ears as she sat with her back pressed against her headboard, mouth agape. She strained to see in the darkness.

Not alone.

Shadows played against the wall where her alarm clock shone dimly. Rheeta could make out human forms filling her bedroom, surrounding her. The temperature dropped.

Thank you.

Weights landed on her bed in multiple spots. She screamed and couldn't untangle herself from the blanket.

We come.

Rheeta felt hands pressing her down, into the bed, icy tendrils surrounding her as her lungs constricted with her breath leaving.

We are welcome.

TWENTY-TWO
#GIRLMOM

Being a traditional wife was amazing. Being a Girl Mom would be epic.

Nia had gotten a nearly indescribable, giddy rush from having reached her first hundred thousand followers. She hadn't been prepared for that rare high to be overshadowed by the way her heart fluttered that first night at the sight of the two sets of Afro puffs bobbing up and down when she asked, "Are you girls hungry?"

Her audience loved her content because she was authentic. They applauded her honest displays of life as a trad wife. The show where she'd broken down and tearfully informed them she couldn't conceive had generated record views.

The only thing that would make their family whole and grow her audience exponentially was sweet babies. Little Joy and Faith would photograph perfectly, their wide, round, brown faces framed by thick hair pulled up into high puffs, showcasing long lashes and huge dark eyes.

Her Mommy content would push her into the higher streaming numbers she needed.

"Hello, Mrs. Timmons," the caseworker said at Nia's front door when she brought the girls to their forever home. The woman's eyes darkened briefly. "Joy and Faith have never stayed with any family for too long. They sometimes have…" she faltered, eyes darting between the little girls who eyed her silently and Nia, who waited patiently for her to finish. "…behaviors that cause difficulty."

She looked as if she wanted to say more, but Nia waved the remainder of her confession away with a graceful hand.

"They're just scared, sweet babies who need lots of love and healthy food." She turned to the girls.

"Would you like to see your room?"

The girls remained silent, faces starting to pale; however, the other woman nodded curtly. "Yes, let's see their accommodations."

Nia led them upstairs and opened the door to the large room the sisters would share. The caseworker stood silently at the door while Nia held her breath and watched the girls. She wanted them to love the things in their room as much as she did.

Nia had spent long hours creating the vibrant colors. Each corner of the room held projects she'd shared with her fans. She'd lovingly worked to make renditions of her favorite childhood toys. There were piles of rag dolls with varying shades of brown skin. Hand-painted wooden blocks lay delicately scattered around two easels with canvases and small containers of finger paints. Personalized woven rugs lay next to their two tiny beds. Fluttery paper butterflies danced among glittery stars, and wisps of sparkly ribbon swayed above the beds.

Three-year-old Joy walked slowly over to a butterfly and grabbed it, excitedly babbling to her older sister, "Fay! Bufwy!"

Tears filled Nia's eyes as Faith ran to join her sister, wide smiles on their faces. The older girl promptly pulled the butterfly down and, before Nia could react, broke the paper in half and stuffed one piece into her mouth and the other into Joy's welcoming orifice.

The caseworker gasped and rushed to chastise them, eyes frantic.

Nia stood between her and them and wiped the paper from the girls' mouths. "It won't hurt them–they're all organic materials. They must be hungry."

"Do you have any pets, Mrs. Timmons?"

"We don't. I may get some later, but we don't have any animals yet."

The caseworker barely looked at her as she rushed through the front door. "Probably best if you don't get any," she'd said quietly.

The girls silently consumed the eggplant noodles Nia prepared for them, their brown skin becoming sallower as the night extended. They didn't fight as she tucked them into bed, the nightlights shining on their pale faces. Nia hoped they'd be recovered by the morning when Kurt arrived home from his trip.

The girls looked smaller and sicklier the next morning. Nia dressed them and took them downstairs to wait for Kurt. As they stared at the breakfast she prepared without touching it, she made a note to talk to their new pediatrician about how to ensure they got sufficient nutrients from the vegan diet she planned to feed them.

When Kurt entered the kitchen, Nia placed a smile on her glossed lips and ran to greet her husband. He released her from the brief hug they shared, and Joy and Faith came toward them.

"Who do we have here?" Kurt asked the question with a fake half-smile that Nia hated.

"This is Joy and Faith," Nia responded. Before she could say more, Faith wrapped her little arms and legs around Kurt's lower body and bit him on the thigh. Her little teeth ripped through his slacks, sinking deeply into his skin. As he yelped and tried to shake her off, Faith held on tighter. She bit harder and dribbled his blood onto the kitchen floor, where Joy lapped it up.

Dawning realization hit Nia in mere moments. The color was returning to her daughter's face as Kurt scrambled around the kitchen, pulling at Faith. Kurt's movements grew weaker, and theirs strengthened. She separated the little girl from her husband, and he breathlessly leaned against the counter and mumbled hoarsely, "What the hell is going on here? That little monster attacked me!"

Nia turned to Joy and Faith. "Babies, go into the back yard there and sit at the little table and wait for me."

The girls did as they were told. Nia turned to her husband, who by then was leaning closer to the floor, ashen underneath his full beard. He tried to speak again, but no words came forth.

"You'll be okay. We just have to teach her that biting isn't nice." She knelt beside Kurt. "Or I could call Dr. Allman and let him know you were bitten by our little girl…" She contorted her face into the wide-eyed, slightly puckered, pouty lipped affect her husband loved. Kurt took in a slow, ragged breath and whispered curses.

Her alpha husband would die before he would admit a bite from a little girl took him to the doctor's office. Knowing she was the victor, she pressed a dishcloth to his leg where the bite had already stopped bleeding. "Go on upstairs and lie down. I'll bring you something to eat and a poultice to put on your leg." Kurt grunted, and she left him to attend to the girls.

Out back, Faith held out part of the half-chewed carcass of a large beetle and offered it to Joy. Both girls chewed on their snack and watched Nia approach. Their eyes were wary, tired—but bright with the nourishment they'd finally gotten.

She sat down between them. "You were still hungry?"

They nodded.

"Why didn't you bite me? Or the caseworker?"

"You're the mommy." Joy made the statement plainly and clearly.

Faith further explained. "You love us already. We need you."

Nia took the girls into her arms and glanced through the patio doors, where she saw the bottoms of Kurt's feet, where he lay on the kitchen floor. She'd need to learn new recipes and figure out how to keep them fed well. Daddy would, aptly, be their first provider.

The board members of his company wouldn't object to him working from home indefinitely. She'd figure out what to do after that when the time came for her to publicly announce a more serene death for him than the one sure to come.

Being a trad widow would be martyrdom. Being a Girl Mommy would be iconic.

TWENTY-THREE
LET'S GO HOME

Lottie loved her elevator. It was extra fancy for other people, but it was a necessity for us to get Lottie from floor to floor in our house. That she loved it and wasn't afraid of it was a bonus.

Every weekday morning, she and I wheeled into the elevator so I could get her to her school bus out front. She giggled loudly and waved her arms with glee. Neither her specialized medical team, nor I, could tell how much vision she actually had, but I did know she always focused her amusement-lit eyes on the back right corner of the elevator.

She laughed the entire ride down and remained focused on that corner as I rolled her out, the beginnings of a frown marking her pretty little face at our leaving. When I'd remind her that we'd be using it again in the afternoon when she got home from school, she'd perk up again and hold her gaze on that back right corner until I closed the door.

The first time she waved her hand purposefully was as we entered her beloved elevator one morning. She raised her right arm up to her eye level and slowly lifted her fingers.

"Are you waving, Lottie? You're so awesome! Look at Mommy's girl."

I was beside myself with excitement. Physical movements were difficult for my baby, but she worked hard to do what she could. I was so proud of her and her determination.

She giggled at my excitement. Her arm dropped. She raised it again, at a diagonal, the way she did when she wanted to rest her hand or arm on me to get my attention. She pointed her hand directly at that back right corner. Her arm stopped, as if her hand had encountered something solid. That something solid wasn't me or the elevator walls. The mirth in her eyes intensified, and a shiver rolled down my arms.

I looked into the corner, which was directly next to where I stood when we rode down. I saw nothing except the wood paneling that made up the elevator walls.

My unease grew as I watched Lottie hold her arm up in that same position the entire ride down. She didn't have the muscle strength to do that unassisted.

That afternoon, she and I stood for a long moment in front of the elevator before I opened the door for our ride up to her room. Lottie signaled her impatience with my hesitance by fidgeting in her chair. When she started to whimper, I knew I couldn't wait any longer. I opened the elevator door and watched my daughter for her response.

As I expected, her eyes again lit up, and she raised her hand, pointing to the back right corner. As we entered, I, too, peered at the corner, looking for anything to explain her amusement and the prickly anxiety that crept over me. I really wanted an explanation for her sudden ability to hold her arm up for such sustained periods of time.

I saw nothing.

Lottie cooed as she closed her outstretched hand, mid-air.

I closed the door, and we started up.

The light went out in the elevator.

I muffled my shriek so I wouldn't scare Lottie. I needn't have worried about Lottie being scared, though. She waved her arms more frantically, laughing herself into breathlessness. A dim, bluish light evolved in the right corner, and a slight movement off to my right side caught my eye.

A little girl was in the elevator with us, someone I had never seen before. She held Lottie's outstretched hand and laughed with as much amusement as Lottie expressed.

I couldn't hear her, but I could see her. She and my baby were enjoying each other. They ignored me as they apparently had done for some time, caught up in their usual elevator play with each other.

The cold I'd felt spread through my whole body. Lottie seemed unaffected by the chill. The elevator ride to the second floor took longer than usual. Then it hit me.

The power was out. We shouldn't have been moving at all.

We weren't going to the second floor.

The moment the realization came, the little girl turned to me and stared straight into my eyes. She then released Lottie's hand to make a brushing motion, sliding her palms together.

"Let's go home," she signed. I recognized the phrase from Lottie and my attempt to learn ASL to see if it was something Lottie could use to communicate. Lottie also remembered the phrase and giggled loudly, nodding her head.

The elevator continued to rise, holding Lottie, me, and the other little girl. It grew colder and colder. The last conscious thought I would have brought warmth to a small corner of my heart at the sight of the two little girls, giggling, singing, and playing together.

They were happy.

We were going home.

TWENTY-FOUR
A WHOLE NEW WORLD

Marika wished her usually brusque mother didn't save all her softness for any time her daughter wanted to leave their house alone. Short, sharp statements that ached a little, she could bear and ultimately ignore. The overly emotional, smothering hugs and the pleading—those were harder to endure.

"Why must you go to these people's house, dearest?" The soft words sounded almost foreign to Marika. Up until she had turned twenty, she avoided leaving the house unless Mama was with her. She had been home-schooled, and that suited her fine. She started college and completed her bachelor's degree completely online.

Now she wanted a little more experience. She applied to a graduate program at the local university and was accepted. All she needed was the money to pay for the classes. She dared not seek funding through work as a teaching assistant or course facilitator. That was a step too far and would require her to be away from the house for long hours at a time, every day. But she had to find her own solutions to payment. Her sweet mama worked so hard to take care of the two of them. Marika would put no heavier burden on her to pay for the rest of her education, nor shock her with her unexpected, prolonged absence before she had to start classes.

She sighed, trying to retain her patience. Her mother didn't mean to cause her stress, even if that's what typically happened in those cases. "Mama, that's usually how babysitting goes. These people live in the 'burbs. They aren't bringing their children here for me to watch them." She gestured at their cozy little inner-city shotgun house, clean but time-worn. She planted a kiss on her mother's cheek and tried to disentangle herself from the cloying embrace.

Her mother sniffed and shook her head, her thick, glossy locs gently swaying with her motion. "You can't just be all up in everybody's house. You can't eat they food, or use their bathroom. Their energy might not be right. It could affect you badly."

Marika grew up with her mother telling her she was special and that various regular experiences could "affect her badly." This did wonders for her self-esteem, especially considering it had only been the two of them for years. No co-parent. No extended family. But this special designation also bothered Marika. What was so special about her? Sure, she was easy to look at, a darker-skinned, carbon copy of her mother. She was also pretty smart, but that was bound to be the result of focused one-on-one home lessons from her equally smart mother.

She also had a preternatural ability to just know things, without understanding how she knew them. But then, she could move things sometimes without touching them, if she concentrated really hard. She didn't see much use for that particular gift of hers very often, except when cleaning up. Surely other people could do these things, too? Her mother could. And she talked as if it was a regular ability to have.

Marika gently pulled away from her mother and kissed her on her still smooth cheek. "I'll be fine, Mama." Then she rushed out the door to the waiting rideshare.

Thankfully, her driver wasn't a chatty one, and she had time to think before she got to the Robbins' home. The older she got, the more weary she grew of being the only child to a single parent. She was twenty years old and wanted to see some of the world. She wanted experiences like dating and parties. She hadn't quite clicked with her online classmates during her classes, and she tended to only interact with them for class purposes. She rarely went anywhere else, where she could come into contact with other people her age. Any time she went to the grocery store, she was with her mother. And as kind and sweet as the older woman was inside, to the outside, she wore a battle-worn expression that didn't invite conversation or friendship.

She hadn't expected the guilt that would come with her desires for freedom. Her father had passed away when she was five years old. She remembered him as a heavy-set man with a lush beard who always smiled when her mother was usually solemn. They matched one another as well as her young child's mind could determine. After his death, her mother never dated again. She didn't have friends who would come and whisk her away to the shopping mall or girl dinners or trips—Marika was her whole world.

Marika didn't want to leave her mother all alone. She also didn't want to spend the rest of her days in their house, puttering around with their herbs and crystals and ancestral altars. That was all fine, and it comforted Marika, knowing she was surrounded by love on the physical plane and the spiritual one. She just wanted to see what else was in the world beyond their home, beyond their small, two-woman circle.

The driver drove through several subdivisions and passed a number of large houses. Finally, he pulled up in front of one with a well-designed yard and facade. The one-story home took up a lot of ground, and the curb appeal made the most of that feature. Marika thanked him and walked up the walkway, fighting sudden shyness all the way.

"Hi. I'm your sitter, Marika." She studied the pair who opened the door to greet her.

"Hi! Glad you made it okay. The directions can sometimes be confusing," The tall, lanky man said with a wide smile. He wore his hair low-cut, and he held a casual sports jacket which he quickly pulled on.

"Oh, we're so happy you came!" The woman exclaimed, teetering on six-inch heels that didn't really make her very tall. Her curly ringlets bounced on her shoulders. "Can I get you something to drink?"

"No, thank you," Marika responded. Their home was cavernous. It could have easily held five of her own home inside it. She tried not to seem out of place in the face of such opulence. The Robbins looked to be not much older than she, yet they already owned this castle of a home.

She was further behind on adulting goals than she had previously thought.

"Well, you're completely welcome to anything in the fridge." The woman looked at Marika full on and wrinkled her eyebrows. "Ah. Are you twenty-one yet?"

"No, not yet."

The woman shook her finger good-naturedly. "Well, we'll keep the bar locked, then, yeah?"

Marika found it strange that the woman would offer her alcohol while she was supervising her children, but she gave no response. She knew through her endless reading that rich people could be a little peculiar, with habits completely unknown to the rest of the world, especially to people who lived isolated lives like Marika.

She followed Mrs. Robbins along a side hallway of the home. The woman put her finger to her lips and gently opened one door. Marika peered in and saw a slight bulge underneath a thick comforter. The small figure was almost too small for the large bed.

"The kiddos are already in bed sleeping, so please don't wake them. They'll sleep through until we return around midnight."

Marika nodded and followed her to a second room, where they repeated their actions and her warning.

They went back to the living room. "We shouldn't be back much later than 11:30 or midnight," Mr. Robbins promised as they walked through the garage door.

"Have fun! And remember, you're welcome to anything you'd like."

"Thank you. Enjoy your evening," Marika replied.

"Yo, yo, yo! Welcome back to your fave, the Robbins' Hood. It's me, Dan, and my partner in wine and crime, Letty Robbins."

Letty waved and dangled a wine glass between her fingers. "And this wine is especially good tonight. You know why?" She nodded toward her husband and gave him a sip from her glass.

"Why?"

They both faced the camera and intoned together, "Because tonight we pull the prank of the century!"

Through bales of laughter, they explained.

Dan started. "We got a sitter tonight for our two children, so we could come out and have a good time."

"The gag is…we don't have any children!" Letty giggled. "You all, our faithful followers, know this. But the darling babysitter does not."

"We're gonna go back home to look for these non-existent kids, and when there are no kids, the sitter will lose her shit!" Dan laughed so hard he could barely talk.

"And before you all say that's mean, we're still gonna pay the sitter her full fee, afterwards, plus a 25% 'prank fee' if she lets us post her response."

"I do hope she lets us post her reaction. I have a feeling this will be epic!"

Marika checked on the children two more times throughout the night. Neither one had stirred, and she wondered what it must be like to be that young and innocent again and be able to sleep like the dead. Neither bedroom was appointed the way she would think children's rooms would be. There were no toys, no books. The pictures on the wall were generic and lifeless. Mostly colorless. She supposed they could have the color small children needed in a playroom somewhere else in the house, but Marika decided none of that was her business.

She checked the locks on all the doors, attending to something that was in her line of duty to perform. Marika had to keep herself and the children safe until their parents returned home. Anything outside that lane wouldn't get any attention from her.

She hardly slept at night, even when she was home. She definitely would never sleep at strangers' houses, so she instead settled on the couch to do some reading. The book she brought along was a nonfiction account of one woman's graduate school journey. The author traveled to the United States for the first time to work towards her master's degree, and Marika felt a deep kinship with the woman.

She may well have been from a different planet, herself, with her lack of knowledge of the outside world. Sure, she read extensively, and her Mama told her stories about their family. She had unlimited access to the television and internet, but something about the knowledge she could gain from those venues rang hollow, especially the internet. It was difficult to parse through authentic lives and experiences and those cultivated just for online audiences.

The potential for falsities made Marika uncomfortable. She was curious about the lives of other people, but wasn't so desperate to investigate that she wanted to delve into the numerous facades and personalities offered on the web or television. She was especially wary of things labeled as "reality" shows or "honest" depictions. Those were created for visual media and had no depth outside of that value. She could identify the masks and the dramatics and see them for what they were—entertainment. Marika much preferred books, including works of fiction, because even through their invented machinations, they more often evoked the most genuine feelings from her.

She was halfway through the sixth chapter of her book when the Robbins returned.

"Did you have a good night?" Marika asked.

Mrs. Robbins' face was flushed, and she suspected the other woman had had an especially good night.

"We did!" Mr. Robbins responded. "I'm going to check on the little ones, and then I'll get you your pay. What forms of payment do you take, again?"

"They've been quiet all night," Marika reported. "I checked on them, but I haven't heard anything from them. They're still sleeping peacefully." She pulled her backpack over and put her book inside. "And you can pay me however is easiest for you. I have the major apps."

Lettie followed her husband down the hallway.

"Where is Junior?" Dan yelled suddenly from outside one of the bedroom doors. "Where's...oh, God!"

Lettie joined in. "Tempest isn't here, either. Tempest!"

Marika froze, her heart dropping. "What do you mean? They've been in bed all night." She ran to the first bedroom, where Lettie was sobbing and throwing bedding around.

"She's not here. She's not here. Junior! Tempest!"

Marika felt around the bedding frantically. "But, but, they have to be here. They were just here..."

"What did you do to them?" Dan approached her, fire in his eyes.

"Where are our babies?" Lottie continued sobbing.

Marika shrieked and felt herself sliding down the wall, onto the floor. She shook her head and heard nothing else. She crawled to the living room she no longer recognized, and sat in the middle of the floor, still as a stone. "They didn't leave the room all evening, not even to go to the bathroom. I would have seen them. They...they..."

She could no longer feel her body. She continued to babble, clenching large handfuls of her hair in her fists.

Dan joined her in the living room, and he and Lettie burst into hysterical laughter.

"Marika, it's okay. Everything is fine. We played a terrible trick on you."

"Yes, it's just a joke. We didn't think you'd take it so hard. We don't even have..."

"Mommy? Daddy? What's happening?" A little squeaky voice broke through Marika's trance. The three adults turned to the sound where a small girl with tiny, sand colored ringlets stood. She wore tiny pink pajamas with baby rabbits on them and pink bunny slippers.

Standing at her side was a slightly older boy. He rubbed his eyes with hands taken from dinosaur pajama-covered arm holes and shifted his weight between his one bare foot and one covered with a vibrant blue sock.

"What's that screaming?" he asked sleepily. "What's happening, Mommy?"

Dan and Lettie instantly sobered, mouths agape. Lettie took a step towards the children, arm outstretched. She jerked it back violently.

"Who are you?" Dan asked.

"Where did you come from?" Lettie added.

Marika finally stood and grabbed her backpack. It was heavier than she remembered. "See. They're fine. I didn't do anything to them." She moved slowly toward the door, repeating, "They're fine." *They're fine…*

"No, no, no!" Lettie ran toward her. "We don't know these kids. Where did they come from? Did you bring them here?"

Marika turned to look at the pictures on the fireplace mantle. She hadn't noticed them before. Several shots of Dan Sr., Lettie, Tempest, and Dan Jr. adorned the shelf.

"What do you mean? You hired me to babysit your two children." She gestured toward the kids still standing at the end of the hall. Her hand trembled, and she grabbed it with her other one.

"No!" Dan Sr. ran his hands across his head. "We don't know these kids! What's happening here?"

Marika looked from the children to the adults, who still eyed the little ones warily.

"You're silly, Daddy. We're your kids," the boy spoke with a grin. "I'm Daniel Jr., and this is my sister Tempest."

"Yeah. You're our mommy and daddy." The little girl's facial expression chilled Marika to her core. Almond-shaped brown eyes held no emotion. No sleep. No…life. She backed up steadily until she reached the front door.

"Wait! Don't leave us here with them!" Lettie called behind her.

Marika ran as fast as she could, out of the yard, out of the subdivision. She didn't stop running until she reached a gas station. She fumbled with her phone, unfamiliar to her, until she could call a rideshare to pick her up and take her home.

Home. When the driver stopped in front of their destination, Marika frowned in confusion. This wasn't her home. The driver watched expectantly, and Marika got out of the car. As it drove off, she slowly walked up the pathway to a small cottage.

She trembled. The door opened, and her mother appeared in the doorway. She ran out to wrap Marika up in a tight hug. A large figure followed behind her and swept the both of them up into his embrace.

"Dearest. I told you to be careful going to folks' houses," her sweet mama crooned as she rocked her.

"Come on inside, beloveds." The man's voice was as jovial as she had remembered. His lush beard sat underneath full lips, slightly smiling.

"Yes, let's go inside," her mother agreed. "We have to figure out how to live in this new world you've created for us, Marika."

"It's a whole new world." Her father intoned the words, and he and his wife led their daughter into their home.

TWENTY-FIVE
WITNESS BEARER

Mama always called me nosy, which is crazy because I only had one nose. She should have called me "eyes" since I had, at last count, a couple thousand of those.

She also could have probably called me a murderer, but she didn't.

I was born with only two eyes on each side of my face. I know this because my first photo album had plenty of nakey pics with me in every pose imaginable. I was the only one in the photos. It had only been me and Mama for as long as I could remember. When I was really little, I asked her once what had happened to my daddy, and she gazed off into the distance and mumbled something I didn't quite understand. As I grew older, I realized whatever had happened had to have been between the ages of two and three. That's when pics of me always with a shirt on started to appear in the later albums.

Years passed, and I finally pieced together the events that had led to his leaving. The eye at the bottom of my right rib cage told me the whole story once I was able to understand. That was his.

Mama and I kept to ourselves in our own little world for those first few years. Eventually, I did have to go to school so Mama could go to work, though. I met my kindergarten teacher and thought I'd love school. Her gaze bore into mine, and my idyllic first day ended with me in burning, itching pain at the lower corner of my left shoulder blade. The pain simply throbbed when I got home, and Mama rubbed it and put some oil on it.

The next day, Mama dropped me off early, and I went into my classroom where the teacher was already waiting. The burning intensified, and I moaned out loud, staggering to my knees. The teacher ran over to where I stood and grabbed me by the shoulders, shaking me violently. The beads at the end of my meticulous braids rattled against each other in my ears.

"What are you doing to me? Why are you here?" She repeated the questions over and over again until my head spun. My pain stopped and the teacher fell to the floor. Images poured into my brain, of the teacher, holding various puppies and kittens underneath the water inside a filled sink. I wanted to cry out in anguish, but I couldn't. The images played until I noticed the teacher wasn't on the floor anymore. Where I first felt pain, I now felt movement underneath my little flower-printed blouse. I stood in the middle of that room, trying to feel what it was. Other kids started coming in, and finally, the principal came, looking for the teacher. She asked if we had seen her or knew where she went. I kept quiet, not wanting to tell any lies. It wasn't a lie that I didn't know where she went. I suspected, but I really didn't know.

Once I arrived home and told Mama what had happened, she raised my shirt to take a look. I couldn't see her face, but I felt the whoosh of her loud intake of air. She put my shirt down and hugged me close to her, my shirt bunched up between her sand-brown arms. Mama homeschooled me after that.

When I was sixteen, I developed a crush on a boy who lived down around the lake from us, who had just moved in with his grandmother to help care for her. I only had five extra eyes at that time, all easily covered by my clothes. Mama and I stayed indoors after having moved to a small, mountainous town where we didn't have to interact with others much, so I had very few opportunities to grow more eyes.

I met the boy in the woods when I went exploring for my science project that Mama assigned. We talked a little that first day. I ignored the burning sensation that time because it was high on my thigh and I didn't know if it was from my desire for him or the other kind. We made a game where we would each sit behind two trees that were relatively close together and talk from there. As long as I wasn't looking at him, there was no pain. Only longing. After the second day, he asked if I could meet him in a more secluded part of the woods so we could really get to know each other.

I read a lot, even though I didn't watch much television. I saw things on the internet. I knew what he meant by that. I wanted him, too. So I met him on the third day. He had a blanket spread out and juice boxes in a bowl. Our eyes met, and I stumbled, my thigh on fire. He helped me to the blanket, and I lay down beside him. He tilted my chin up so we could be face-to-face. We didn't even make it to first base. The bewildered look on his face replaced the teenage horniness and then morphed into terror. He backed away from me.

"Stop it! Stop it!" he screamed.

"You stop it!" I didn't want the images I saw emanating from him. Him slapping his grandmother hard across the face. Him pouring boiling water on her feet as she lay prone in her bed. Him climbing on top of her, between her legs, raping her. Over and over again.

I knew the pictures were truth. My anger made me hold my gaze on him and watch as he began to swirl around like paper confetti in a windstorm. I opened my legs and welcomed the relief of pain as the person confetti dissipated and the familiar movement started on my thigh. I got up off the blanket and went home. I didn't have many boyfriends after that.

I'm a witness bearer. It is my duty to bear witness to the injustices I encounter and take their stories into my being. They develop into eyes, judges for the following injustices. There's always more wrongdoing.

I have one eye I treasure most. I call it my Mama Eye. It's different because it was conceived willingly, borne of an unbreakable bond of love. When I turned twenty, Mama called me into the bath-room where she lay in a pinkish tub of water.

"I can't protect you here in the flesh, mine beloved," she whis-pered. Her wrists pumped out her life's blood into the pool around her.

"Mama! No! Don't leave me!" I felt the familiar burning, this time at the corner of my left breast. Right above my heart. I understood. I took off my shirt and bra and held Mama, cooing comfort to her and relishing in the growth of my Mama Eye.

"I will always be with you." She took a final breath, and I watched the eye open. It was the most beautiful eye I had ever seen. It told me the story of Mama's sickness, the cancer that ate her alive. It whispered to me of her pain and her desire to remain with me forever. The injustice of her pain and impending death was recorded within me forever.

I remained alone after her death, venturing out only at night. My dark brown skin and the heavy clothing I wore concealed most of the eyes. The others, I could play off as tattoos, as long as no one stared too long. Those who did stare often did so because their eye was burgeoning and they couldn't resist their destiny. Once I started encountering more people, the eyes developed almost every day.

This is my calling. I embrace it. I make a good living with Mama's life insurance payout and as a hermit writer, enclosing verbiage in all my contracts that I'll only ever be a ghostwriter and never have my name listed on any of my works. No press, no inter-views, no appearances. My agent didn't care as long as she continued to get paid.

I have a girlfriend now, too. Sheba. The first time I showed her my eyes, she stared at me in awe. Lovingly, she kissed each and every one, asking it to tell her its story sometime. She started with my Mama Eye, paying homage to my beloved mother and asking her permission to love me. My Mama Eye agreed, closing to the inti-macy that followed. And the eyes started telling her their stories.

I tell Sheba she's good for me, that I need her. Once I opened myself fully to her, each eye that told her its story then melted away, leaving behind a tingling and an opening for a new eye. At each dissolution, Sheba whispers ancient phrasings, and the story is gone. She continues to ask, and the stories are told. The eyes go away.

I'm the witness bearer, and she's the absolution. She's my soulmate.

ACKNOWLEDGMENTS

For me, writing doesn't happen in a bubble. It takes place from the corner of an entire horror village. Supporting me are my family, my closest friends, and my fellow authors. My agent, Natasha Mihell, and publisher, Cassandra Thompson, are critical parts of my village, as are the readers who help keep my work alive by reading and talking about it.

This book doesn't exist without all of you. Thank you for your unwavering support.

ABOUT THE AUTHOR

R. J. Joseph is a Bram Stoker Awards® Winner and a Shirley Jackson nominated, Texas-based writer/speaker/editor. Her creative and academic work examines the intersections of race, gender, and class in the horror genre and popular culture. She occasionally peeks out on various social media platforms from behind @rjacksonjoseph or at www.rhondajacksonjoseph.com.

THANK YOU FOR READING

Thank you for reading *My Monsters Ain't Like Yours*. We deeply appreciate our readers, and are grateful for everyone who takes the time to leave us a review. If you're interested, please visit our website to find review links. Your reviews help small presses and indie authors thrive, and we appreciate your support.

More Women's Horror from Quill & Crow

Ending in Ashes, Rebecca Jones Howe

The Stitch Witches, Krissie K. Williams

Bed Rot Baby, Wendy Dalrymple

TRIGGER INDEX

Abuse of women (emotional/physical/sexual)

Bigotry (misogyny, racism)

Body Horror

Cannibalism

Child Abuse/Child Sexual Abuse (Chapter 19)

Child Death

Death/Murder

Slavery

REPRINT INFORMATION

"#GirlMom," produced February 2024 by *Something Scary Podcast*

"Endless Possibilities," published July 13, 2023 by Hungry Shadow Press in *The First Five Minutes of the Apocalypse*

"Her Heart's Desire," published May 2022 by AEA Publishing in *Shattered and Splintered*

Bram Stoker Awards® Winner for Superior Achivement in Short Fiction: "Inheritance," published March 2025 by Uncomfortably Dark in *Full Throttle, A Dark Dozen Anthology.*

"Let's Go Home," produced February 2023 by *Something Scary Podcast*

"No Tricks, Only Treats," produced October 2022 by *Something Scary Podcast*

"Regrets Never Die," published October 2021 by Keith Anthony Baird in *Diabolica Americana: A Dark States Horror Compendium*

"Sad, Spooky Sally," published August 4, 2023 by Encyclopocalypse in *Legends and Lore*

"Skinny Minnie," produced February 2022 by *Something Scary Podcast*

"Suffer the Little Children," published February 2022 by Dark Dispatch in *Winter 2022 Issue*

"The Collector," published February 25, 2022 by Kandisha Press in *Slash-Her*

"The Crazy with Daisy," published May 3, 2022 by Cemetery Gates Media in *Picnic in the Graveyard*

"The Preying Family," published November 7, 2023 by The Seventh Terrace in *Solstice in Purgatory*

"Those Who Teach Pay Knowledge Forward," published September 19, 2023 by Shortwave Publishing in *Wilted Pages: An Anthology of Dark Academia*

"Welcome," published October 2023 by midnight&indigo in *midnight&indigo: Eighteen Speculative Stories by Black Women Writers, Volume III*

"Where the Horizon Meets the Sky," published November 8, 2022 by Black Spot Books in *Into the Forest: Tales of the Baba Yaga*

"Witness Bearer," published February 2021 by Sci Fi and Scary in *Twisted Anatomy: SF & S Body Horror Anthology*